Ribbon

Of

River

ROSE MARIE SHAW

Cover Design by Cecelia Morgan

Dedicated to my ancestors

PREFACE

Dindley was a sleepy hamlet where life carried on monotonously with season after season of routine, and any diversion from the humdrum existence was regarded with great excitement. Today was one of those days and inquisitive villagers, absent from their work, came out of their homes and crowded the drovers' road. The alehouse, where today even the women were allowed inside to witness justice being done, was filled to capacity. Those at the back of the room and in the doorway jostled and pushed with their elbows to get a better view of this extraordinary event.

The constable, the rector and two parish councillors, all dressed in their official outfits, were assembled to adjudicate the meeting and sat squeezed shoulder to shoulder on a settle along one wall. A long discussion had carried on between them as to the format the court of law should follow. There were to be two hearings today, the second one was of such great importance that they may not be sufficiently competent to deal with it. A table in front of them was covered with official looking papers listing rules and regulations as a guidance to aid the proceedings.

'Can we start with the case of Mrs Ada Dawson and Mrs Saunders each accusing the other of assault? Can they be brought to the front?'

The two women were pushed forward from somewhere in the middle of the crowded room, each with a defiant glare at the other and protesting loudly at being manhandled. The outcome of an argument which had got out of hand was now the basis of their court appearance and they continued to quarrel as they stood in front of the table.

'Silence!' demanded the constable. 'You're like a pair of fishwives. Mrs Dawson, we'll hear from you first.'

'Yes. On Wednesday I went to her house,' she said, pointing at Mrs Saunders, 'and asked for the money she owed me for the bread I'd baked and my son had delivered to her house over the past two weeks. She wouldn't give me the money and called me a rogue because she said I'd charged her for bread she hadn't had. I hadn't charged her too much and we had a row and she hit me in the face.'

'I didn't hit her,' interrupted Mrs Saunders. 'It was her that hit me. She was in a bad temper and she hit me calling me a low, wicked woman.'

The two parish councillors agreed this was a paltry matter for such a court and referred to the rector, asking if he would agree to administer more worthwhile religious guidance to the two women. The rector nodded his approval and called it a disgraceful, sinful thing that neighbours could not live in peace. The bench agreed that the case, being a thing of no consequence, be dismissed and the second investigation of considerably more importance be started. They requested that maybe before the proceedings began and they laid blame and passed judgement, they be given some background to this unfortunate situation.

It had all started the day the letter arrived. Four horses in front of the mail coach were pulled to a halt at the head of the valley where the road forks. A fine sight; the distinctive scarlet and gold livery shone in the sun, the driver sat on the high seat, and the guard at the rear cradled a blunderbuss. As soon as the children heard the post horn they ran up the drovers' road, losing no speed, until they reach the highroad. There would be money to be made, holding the horses' reins or carrying luggage. There was nobody waiting to get on the coach and nobody got off; there was just one letter to be delivered, so they would be unlucky today.

The coachman looked for the oldest and brightest of the children.

'You, boy, what's your name?'

'Bobby Saunders, sir.'

'Do you know which is Mr Fothergill's house?'

'Yes, sir.'

'Can you run?'

'Yes, sir, I can run fast.'

The coachman climbed down, stretching his aching body wearied by the long journey and handling the heavy reins, and made his way to the rear of the coach, glancing again at the boy to determine whether he was to be trusted. He rummaged through the post box and handed Bobby the letter to be delivered in the village. The boy stood his ground, staring at the driver in silent plea, and did not move until a penny was tossed through the air for him to catch.

Arncombe,
Herefordshire.

March 30, 1824

Algernon, My Dear Nephew,

I thank you for your considerate letter which I received some time ago and apologise for having been so long with my reply. This is due to the unforeseen occurrences of the past weeks which has kept me well away from my writing desk and many other obligations. Neither can I, at the moment, give you my opinion of your new book which you kindly sent to me. In truth, it is still unwrapped and awaits my attention but my curiosity flourishes and will soon take over.

First may I enquire of your health? I was distressed that you wrote, indeed lamented, that the demands of your work at the school have become tiresome. This is unusual as previously you always thrived on your duties of education. The years are no longer kind to you and I, and we must avoid overburdened long hours into the night for fear of depression of the mind. You should consider seeking extra help at the school and ease the fatigue you are experiencing. The winter has been unyielding and maybe a vacation to a warmer climate, at least until the summer is upon us, would suit your temperament better.

As you know I have been warden to Lizzie now for the past four months, with no hardship on my part, may I add. Despite all my endeavours she has little improved in her mind from the traumatic event which shocked us all. The effect of the terror still invades her sleep and I sit at her bedside late into the night. Her wounds healed quickly enough but grief always grips the young for the longest time. We all pray for her that she may soon find contentment again but I fear the images will stay with her for the rest of her life.

Today she became thirteen years old and I am at a loss to know

4

what to do. I must find her a suitable position with a sympathetic employer. She is reasonably intelligent and keeps herself clean and tidy, but needs someone who would be mindful of her tragic circumstances and who would treat her with compassion. Do you know of such a person?

I am unable to take her into my employ, being no longer of an age to enjoy youthful company. I must favour Agnes who has looked after me sufficiently for many a year. She is very loyal and an extra pair of hands might cause a misunderstanding between us.

Finally I come to the end of my letter and thank you for your timeless invitation to visit with you at your home in Dindley. It is with the regret that I am unable to accept. Although the Yorkshire air might be conducive to my well-being I think the long journey would be too arduous for me and detrimental to my health.

I remain your affectionate Aunt,

Miss Dorothea Fothergill

Chapter 1

It had been a long, hot day and Lizzie was eager to finish the cooking and let the fire die down. She mopped her brow with the corner of her apron but the starched cotton scratched her face and did little to relief her discomfort. Water boiled around the large joint of bacon in the blackened iron kail pot which hung from the crane above the range fire, and the dining room was set out ready the way Mr Fothergill liked it. When the meal was eaten she could tidy everything away and maybe have an hour to herself before retiring to her bed.

The evening air still held the heat of the July day. The fields around the village were void of workers, who had wearily made their way home, scythes and rakes resting on slumped shoulders, haymaking done for the day. Cottage chimneys smoked as fanned flames radiated heat to cook the evening meal.

Philanderers, poachers, drunks and gamblers, deceivers and the foolhardy lived among the god-fearing people of Dindley where incest and interbreeding over many years had unwittingly added to the problems of the close-knit community.

It was a small village nestled in the flat lowlands on the south side of a Yorkshire dale in the north of England where a river, fed by tributaries running off the boggy moors, became fast flowing. The main street was a well-worn and grooved drovers' track where horse-drawn wagons rolled through the village and then on ten miles to Hawes, the nearest market town. The surrounding land was fertile and horses and cattle grazed contentedly in lush pastures. Hens scratched and pecked at the sides of grassy tree-lined lanes, and hedgerows produced fruit and nuts which provided food for many a hungry villager. Houses and barns, solidly built with the local millstone grit and stout oak frames, stood proudly along the river bank. Close to the church, their long gardens full of vegetables, herbs and flowers were labourers' cottages; homes full of laughter and hope, sometimes tears and tragedy, many with secrets to take to the grave or maybe maliciously revealed.

In the front parlour, waiting to see Mr Fothergill, Reuben Webster stood, cap in hand. He was uncomfortable in such fine surroundings and paced the floor from door to window. A big clock hung on the wall and thumped rhythmically; the awesome ticking like a heartbeat with each swing of its long pendulum. Reuben took a deep breath as he felt the beating in his chest. There were chairs large enough to sleep in and polished fire irons lay on the big hearth. Rows of leather-bound books, some written by Mr Fothergill himself, were neatly displayed on shelves in alcoves. A white goose-feather quill protruded from an inkwell on a fine inlaid wooden writing desk. The pervasive aroma of pastry and bacon coming from the kitchen was overpowering to Reuben, who had not eaten all day and it made the waiting even more arduous.

'Mr Webster, what brings you here at this late hour? I was just about to have my supper,' said Mr Fothergill as he appeared in the parlour doorway, holding on to the doorknob to make it obvious he was displeased at the intrusion.

'I am sorry, Mr Fothergill, sorry to disturb you,' Reuben said, twisting his cap in his hands and swallowing the saliva invading his mouth.

'Have you come here looking for work?'

'Er, hmm, no, Mr Fothergill.'

'Are you in work at the moment?'

'Yes. I'm hired by the squire and helping with the haymaking.'

'Are you finding your employment satisfactory?'

'Aye, it's well enough.'

'Well then, what is it you want? Get on with it, spit it out. Lizzie's waiting to serve my supper,' he said, still maintaining his position in the doorway ready to show Reuben out.

'I was given a letter this morning. Nobody ever sends me letters so it must be important. I can't understand it and I would like you to read it and explain it to me.'

'A letter to you, eh?'

'Aye. A man rode all the way over from High Harrogate with it. Brought it up to squire's top field where I was working so as to give it me personally.'

'My word, give it to me. Let me see,' Mr Fothergill said, his interest aroused. Letting go of the doorknob he walked into the room with an outstretched hand. Reuben took a crumpled piece of paper from his pocket and passed it across the desk. Mr Fothergill unwrinkled the document and walked over to the big bay window, held it up towards the last of the evening light then studied it for some time.

'Well I never,' he said, looking at Reuben, back at the letter, then at Reuben again.

'Whatever is it?' Reuben asked.

'It's a will, Reuben. Widow Learoyd's will. There's a part of it that concerns you. I'll read it out to you:

'This day in the year of the Lord Eighteen Hundred and Twenty Eight I give and bequeath the dwelling house known as Townsend Cottage in the parish of Dindley, in the North Riding of the county of Yorkshire. Also the land being thirty acres known as North Fell, with moorland grazing and sheep thereon, to Reuben Webster, son of my lifelong friend John Webster deceased, to be his during his lifetime and to his heir, possession only from the day he takes unto him a wife.'

Reuben did not speak. He stood open-mouthed and with a frown of curiosity. North Fell was rough moorland across the river on the north side of the dale, and an area he was not familiar with. A stone packhorse bridge, the humpback spanning the river at its narrowest point, was the only crossing. From the bridge a steep, narrow lane, overgrown and unused, led to North Fell. The incline gradually converted to heather moorland where sheep freely roamed among outcrops of weatherworn crags; the landscape quilted with dry stone walling and peppered with boulders which had broken away and lay where they had landed. Townsend Cottage, which was to become Reuben's home, but only if he married, perched precariously on the isolated hillside a good two miles from the village.

'Do you not understand?' asked Mr Fothergill.

'Well, yes, but why would she leave all that land to me? I was nothing to her.'

Reuben collapsed into one of the big chairs then, remembering his place, quickly stood up again.

'Have you any plans to marry?' asked Mr Fothergill, moving away from the light of the window and inviting him to return to the comfort of the vacated armchair.

'No, I'm never going to get wed. I've got nought to offer a wife.'

'You have now. A farm, a cottage and goodness knows how many sheep there are up on North Fell.'

Reuben imagined himself walking on the moor amongst his sheep. His very own sheep. Already he was planning what would need attending to. He fidgeted excitedly in the confines of the big armchair and tried to restrain the giggling welling up inside him.

'I'd best get up there on North Fell tomorrow first thing. Those sheep will need shearing.'

'No, Reuben, the will says you inherit when you marry. You cannot touch them until you marry.'

'But I have no one in mind. Any road, who'd have me?'

He did not have to look far. Unbeknown to the two men, Lizzie had crept into the passage and was eavesdropping outside the door. She had heard every word. *What a wonderful opportunity this is for me,* she thought, *the likes of which may never come my way again. Marriage, mistress of my own home and a family instead of just being a servant.*

She would always remember her childhood home. Happy evenings when the family sat round the fire and looked for pictures in the flames. Her father telling wonderful stories, and then all four children cuddling up together in one big bed, sleeping soundly. That had all ended five years ago.

One night when she was twelve years old and they were all asleep in their beds, she dreamed she could see the moon through the roof, the light shining down on her like a blessing from Heaven. It was only when a piece of burning thatch dropped on to the bed and set it alight that she realised it was not a dream. Timbers cracked and the smell of smoke made her cough and choke. Abruptly fully awake she screamed and shouted to wake everyone. With the red-hot floor burning her bare feet she ran outside into the yard. Her nightdress smouldering against her skin added to the pain. She ripped it off and stood naked, still screaming for the others to get out. She remembered seeing her mother, flames lapping round her, trying to climb the stairs to get to the other children. Lizzie waited for them all to get out. She waited and waited but nobody followed her out of the flames. In one night she had lost her entire beloved family. Her mother, two brothers and a sister, and her father whom she loved dearly. Her stalwart father had been her idol, someone she aimed to be like, and after five years she still missed his guidance very much.

She had been in a shocked daze for many days after the fire, but could remember being taken to a house and covered with a blanket. The blanket was soft and smelled of lavender. A very old lady dressed in black, an apparition like a witch, sat silently at her bedside and smeared the burns on her feet with ointments which felt cool and soothing. She remembered the funeral and looking into the grave; a hole in the ground so deep she could not see the bottom. Two large coffins disappeared down and down into it, then three small ones were laid across them. Lizzie cried bitterly as an arm came around her shoulders and led her away. The tears had continued for days, they just would not stop.

As soon as the burns had healed she was lifted on to a seat on top of the mail coach. A long three-day journey passing through woods, towns and villages, through mud and over cobbles, took her away from her home in the west country to Yorkshire where the old lady's nephew, Mr Fothergill, had agreed to employ her.

Mr Fothergill had been good to her during the five years she had worked for him, even though the uniform she had to wear was hideous; he had taken her in when she had nowhere else to go. He had even taught her to read and write and allowed her to read some of his books for which she was eternally grateful, but she had worked hard for him. She had scrubbed floors, swept carpets, lit fires, polished brasses, changed beds and done all the laundry. The house had been run very efficiently and the meals had been cooked to perfection, but now her debt was paid. Marriage would mean that no more would she have to blacken his boots and empty his chamber pot. She could have a family again.

There was no time to waste in pursuing her objective. Lizzie had to get inside the parlour and flaunt herself discreetly in front of Reuben. She quietly took a few steps back down the corridor, coughed, then approached the door again, making her footsteps heard, and knocked as if she had just come from the kitchen.

'Yes, what is it?'

'Your supper, Mr Fothergill, shall I keep it warm?'

'No, Mr Webster is just going. I will be right there.'

'You get your supper, Mr Fothergill, before it gets cold. I'll see Mr Webster to the door,' said Lizzie, seizing the opportunity to be alone with him.

'Leave the will with me, Reuben. I'm going to Low Harrogate tomorrow. I can visit the executor of the will on your behalf. Come back tomorrow after supper and we'll discuss this further.' He offered his hand to Reuben.

'Thank you,' said Reuben, looking at the proffered hand but automatically touching his forelock. Mr Fothergill's hand stayed outstretched. Reuben, who had come straight from working in the fields, was embarrassed by the state of his appearance and looked down at his dirty right hand. He rubbed it on the side of his dusty trousers, making little improvement, then shook hands heartily and followed Lizzie to the front door.

'Good night, Mr Webster,' Lizzie shouted loud enough so that Mr Fothergill, who was now in the dining room tucking into a generous slice of bacon, would hear. Then, with a hooked finger, she beckoned Reuben back and whispered, 'Go round to the back door and I'll give you some bacon for your supper.'

Lizzie ran back through the house to the kitchen, snatching off her cloth cap as she ran and taking the pins from her hair to let her long black curls fall on to her shoulders. She arrived at the back door before Reuben and by the time he had walked round the house and across the yard she was leaning seductively against the door frame, ready to flirt outrageously with him. Unfortunately for Lizzie the only thing Reuben was interested in was the bacon, and as soon as it had been cut from the joint and the bait was in his hand, he was gone, leaving her looking very foolish.

Oh well, she thought, *it takes patience to catch a fish.*

Chapter 2

The long, hot summer was relentless. A good year for haymaking and working in the fields but not for attic bedrooms. The heavy air had been rising to the top of the house all day and that was where Lizzie slept. She had lain awake all night, tossing and turning, uncomfortable not only with the heat but also with thoughts milling around in her head trying to think of a way to attract Reuben's attention.

She had no idea how to attract a man. This was something she had never done before, something she had never previously given much thought to, and she was at a loss as to how to do it but determined that one day soon she would be Reuben's wife. To start with she thought she would have to make herself look appealing. It would be hard to do that when she did not have any pretty clothes, only starched pinafores and two straight shift dresses, no fancy combs to fasten her hair and no white stockings. Her hands were rough and red raw, and her nails were broken and grubby from all the housework.

With sleep still evading her, she stood and looked out of the tiny window of her attic bedroom and watched the big red ball of sun appear above the horizon, bathing the landscape in a pink haze. The black river reflected the rays of light, painting the water with flowing ribbons of blood crossed by a flash of blue as a kingfisher skimmed the surface, already hard at work. In a field she could see a sleepy milkmaid, bucket and stool in hand, trudging towards a lowing cow. The world was waking up, another day beginning, and the routine work starting all over again.

Sometimes if Mr Fothergill had set out early before breakfast to travel to Low Harrogate and the School for Young Gentlemen, which he owned, her day would be more relaxed and she could please herself what to do and what to leave for another day. She would stand at the window, daydreaming. She loved this time of day, the early morning; the quiet before the hustle and bustle of her busy day. There was no mistress of the house for Lizzie to answer to. Mr Fothergill had no inclination to marry so Lizzie was her own mistress. The high fees he unashamedly charged his pupils to board at the school kept him in comfort, and young Lizzie ran his house efficiently and to his liking.

She watched the sun move obliquely across the sky as it slowly changed from red into a glorious blaze of gold. Eclipsed by a big, old oak tree at the bottom of the garden, the light through its branches shone like smouldering embers ready to burst into flame. It reminded her of the fire and her family but she tried to get the image out of her mind. This could be the start of a new chapter in her life. *One day, she thought, when I have my own home, I'll plant an acorn and have an oak tree I can watch growing season after season. The pale-green buds opening in spring, the full regalia in summer, and the snow and frost on the bare branches in winter. It would grow tall and be enjoyed by future generations living in my house.*

Every morning Lizzie tidied her bedroom exactly as Miss Fothergill, or Aunt Dorothea as she liked Lizzie to call her, had taught her. She made the bed and put her nightdress, neatly folded, under the top sheet. After washing her hands and face, quickly because the water poured from the jug was cold but refreshing, she folded the towel and placed it back on the rail. A quick dust round and it was done, ready for inspection although Mr Fothergill had never ventured into her bedroom to check it like Agnes, Aunt Dorothea's housekeeper, used to. The daily routine began straightaway on her way downstairs. Making sure Mr Fothergill was awake and dressed, she would tidy the big bedroom where he slept and carry his chamber pot downstairs to empty outside at the bottom of the garden.

The lack of sleep made her feel lethargic but she made an effort to clean and tidy. The morning dragged on and eventually she had the washing pegged on the line and blowing in the warm breeze, until all she had to do was prepare the vegetables for Mr Fothergill's evening meal ready for when he returned from Harrogate. It was then that an idea came to her; an idea she thought could not fail to attract Reuben. It would be so easy.

There were far more vegetables on the kitchen table than she would need for the evening meal and, still working on the theory that the way to Reuben's heart might be to feed him, and knowing which field he would be working in, decided on her course of action. She cooked carrots, turnip, parsnip, onion, mushrooms and asparagus in the big kail pot. Flavouring came from caraway seeds and the best herbs she could pick from the garden, and she added a little of each until she was satisfied that the vegetables tasted sweet and did not smell too pungent.

While the mixture was still hot she filled a basin, cut a generous knob of butter from the block in the cool dairy and placed it on top, put a spoon in the middle, then wrapped it in a clean cloth. Covering her soiled dress with her best pinafore as it was not yet the day to change into her clean dress, she set off with the food to the field where Reuben was working. She had it all planned in her mind. She would offer him the food thinking he would be so grateful she had thought about him being hungry. She would sit in a quiet corner of the field and talk with him while he ate and she would steer the conversation casually towards the subject of marriage. Not too brazen, just enough to let him know she was more than interested. *A great idea,* she thought, *it can't fail.*

She could feel the heat of the basin in her hands as she ran down the lane and all the way to the hayfields. Lizzie had not expected to see so many people. Men, women and children were hard at work with pitchforks and rakes even though the midday sun was blazing high in the sky. There was no quiet corner anywhere that Lizzie could get Reuben on his own to talk to him. One haystack had been built and thatched. A second one had been started alongside the first.

An old man, no longer able to take part, leaned with drooped shoulders on a fence and filled his long clay pipe with tobacco. With tired, watery eyes he watched the youngest of the children playing tig round the haystacks. It was a long time since Lizzie had played games like hide-and-seek and catch-me-if-you-can. She was tempted to join in but today she had to be the lady, act grown up and responsible. All the men wore wide-brimmed hats to protect them from the sun's glare, which made it hard to recognise who they were.

She could not see Reuben and had to ask the old man if he knew which one he was. He took the clay pipe from his mouth, turned his head, and spat a fountain of tobacco-stained saliva on the ground before pointing with the stem of his pipe to the second haystack. Reuben was perched on top, raking the hay into position to form the second stack. Waving positively to him she held the basin high so that he would see that she had brought him something. To Lizzie's delight he put down his rake, slid down the side of the stack, and ran across the field towards her. But unfortunately for Lizzie, it was not to enjoy her company. It was because he thought it must be something urgent; maybe Mr Fothergill was back from seeing the executor in Harrogate and had a message for him about the will and his new-found fortune.

'Hello, Mr Webster. I've come to tell you that Mr Fothergill is expecting you to visit him tonight after you have finished your work.'

'Is that all you have to tell me? No news?'

'No, no news. As I said he is expecting you this evening.'

'Well, I know that. I arranged it with him myself, to visit at whatever time I was finished with the day's haymaking,' he said. 'You didn't have to come all this way, interrupting my work, to tell me that. You are a silly girl.'

Feeling belittled at being called silly and alarmed by his abrupt manner, she realised her plan was not working and that she should have thought of a much better excuse for coming to see him. He started to walk away. She had to act fast and ran after him calling to his turned back.

'Mr Webster, Mr Webster. I thought maybe you had forgotten,' she blurted out and quickly thrust the basin toward him. 'Would you like this for your dinner?' she asked.

'What is it?' he asked suspiciously.

'I've just cooked it myself. Maybe we could sit here near the haystack while you eat it and I'll wait for the basin to take back with me.'

'Just leave it there. They need me on the stack. I can't break off until the foreman gives the signal to everyone. We all break together.'

'Oh, all right, I'll sit down here and wait. I have plenty of time, Mr Fothergill has gone to Low Harrogate visiting a gentleman friend and he'll be away most of the day,' she said, but Reuben was gone before she had finished the sentence, leaving her talking to herself and once again feeling very childish.

As she waited, the children grew bored with their games and started rolling about and throwing hay at each other and annoying her. She wished they would go away so she could sit sedately and, with a bit of luck, Reuben would look her way and maybe think she looked a little attractive. Bobby Saunders, a mischievous seventeen-year-old, was peeping round the corner of the haystack shouting and jeering at her.

'Give us a kiss, Lizzie. Go on, give us a kiss,' he taunted.

'I'll give you a clip round the ear. That's all I'll give you, you scallywag.'

He continued to tease her.

'Oh, grow up, you silly little boy,' she said, trying hard herself to be grown up even though she was only one year older than him. There was a big difference between him being seventeen and her being eighteen.

He pulled her hair and threw hay into her face until eventually the annoyance became too much and she lost her self-control. The ladylike composure she was trying so hard to maintain burst into a fit of anger. She put the basin down and jumped up to chase him. As she jumped, her foot knocked the basin over and the herb-flavoured vegetables with caraway seeds spilled over, trickled out, and disappeared through the loose stalks of the hay.

'Now look what you've made me do,' she howled.

She made a grab for him but he was quicker than her and ran away round the corner of the haystack, laughing and cheekily pushing his tongue out at her. Everyone in the field heard the shouting and stopped work to watch the frivolity. The men, including Reuben, laughed heartily and cheered Bobby on. The women, who had heard the quick-spreading rumours that Reuben needed a wife and realised what Lizzie was up to, sneered and tut-tutted.

Humiliated to the point of tears, Lizzie could feel a burning blush rising up her neck into her face and ran from the field shouting, 'I'll get you for this, Bobby Saunders, you see if I don't.'

Chapter 3

A mixture of disappointment and embarrassment had broken Lizzie's spirit. She could not free herself from the humiliation and wished it had all been a bad dream. Day and night she could hear Reuben's cruel, raucous laugh. Blocking her ears with her hands did not make it go away. She could see him, hands on his hips, head thrown back, standing on top of the haystack. She covered her eyes but the image was still there. She had misjudged Reuben to suppose he would be so naïve as to fall for such a trick. It had all been an idiotic fantasy to think that she could be part of his life. She was not unhappy living with Mr Fothergill, she just had this desire erupting inside her for something better in her life and marriage to a man of property seemed to be the answer. It was more than a whimsical fancy, it was a deep feeling she could not explain.

For days she struggled with her work but there was so much housekeeping she left undone. She just pottered in a stupor, making little progress, before shutting herself in her bedroom and curling up on her bed like a dormant cocoon, the frustration turning over and over in her mind. All the things she had dreamed of, schemed for, were not to be. The bare walls and sparse interior of the attic bedroom reflected the emptiness she felt inside. Even the view from the window no longer pleased her.

Mr Fothergill was upset by Lizzie's sudden change of mood. He had not seen this side of her before and could not understand what had changed to make her so reticent.

'Lizzie, is something wrong? Are you not well?' he asked.

Lizzie shrugged her shoulders and looked down at her hands, unable to say how she felt. She wanted to confide in him and explain;

the words were there in her head, but just seemed to vaporize when she tried to speak.

'Am I getting any food today? Speak up, child,' he demanded, impatient at her continued silence, but the sudden command just made Lizzie more distressed.

A deep sense of inadequacy left Mr Fothergill at a loss as to how to handle her. He spread his hands in a gesture of resignation. Should he get angry with her? *No*, he thought, *that won't work. She'll just burst into tears and run back up to her bedroom.* He smacked his forehead with the palm of his hand. Should he try talking logically with her? No, he knew she would not listen. Any boy at his school adopting such a reticent attitude would be thrown into a bath of cold water, but such treatment of course was out of the question for Lizzie. *The best idea*, he thought, *would be for me to pass her on to someone more qualified to deal with these matters.*

'I'll ask the rector to have a word with you,' he said, pulling on the bottom of his waistcoat with a nod of his head and a satisfying, 'Mmm. Maybe he can get to the bottom of all this.'

The Reverend Augustus Sewell was summoned and, always ready to deliver his parishioners from their predicaments, duly arrived, riding on his pony. Lizzie, rescued from the attic, was brought before him in the parlour. He stood near the window, Bible in one hand; the other holding on to his lapel. He looked disapprovingly over his spectacles then asked Mr Fothergill to leave them alone.

'Oh, of course,' said Mr Fothergill, relieved to be out of the equation.

The rector smiled at Lizzie; a false smile which wrinkled his face and showed his brown teeth, then beckoned with his long, crooked finger for her to approach.

'Come, my child. The Devil seems to have possessed your soul and you must pray until the demon is driven out. Kneel, my child, and let us pray together' His eyeglasses pinched the end of his nose so tightly that he spoke with a nasal tone.

Obediently Lizzie knelt in front of him, praying with her hands pressed together as tight as she could and her eyes closed. Although she did take a peek at him with his head thrown back, looking out of the window and up to Heaven. She prayed so hard she thought her heart would burst, but she still did not feel any different; the discontent was still there. Maybe because her prayer had nothing to do with expelling the Devil, but rather asking for Reuben to be sent her way.

'Look well into your Bible, my child,' he said and, with instructions to keep praying, he left. She watched him stride across his pony and ride away into the village, his remuneration jingling in his pocket. The comical black-clad figure sat ungainly astride the pony; greatly undersized to carry such a tall, lanky individual; the brim of his big hat flapping up and down in rhythm with his bouncing body. His stockinged legs protruded from knickerbockers like twigs branching into big feet almost trailing on the ground.

The ludicrous sight amused Lizzie and the corners of her mouth slowly turned up into a smirk. Then a smile, and it was not long before Mr Fothergill heard rousing hymns being sung in the kitchen and he was assured that he had made the right decision by calling for ecclesiastical help. He adjusted his waistcoat in his usual smug manner, delighted with his accomplishment, though not achieved in the way he thought it had been, by the power of prayer. He did not see Lizzie trotting mockingly round the kitchen table as if she were riding a pony. She came to a sudden halt as the door burst open and he was suddenly there in front of her, demanding an explanation of her past conduct.

'Now, Lizzie, what has all this nonsense been about?'

'It was nothing, sir, just a problem I had and I don't want to talk about it. I would just like to forget it.'

'Why did you not address me with this problem? Are you not happy here?'

'Oh yes, sir, very happy.'

'Then what is it? Is it so dreadful that you cannot talk to me about it, child?' he asked, feeling instinctively protective towards her.

'That's just it. I'm not a child. I am old enough to be married and I have a desire to be so.'

The tiresome moniker 'child' angered Lizzie and the impetuous outburst relieved her of the embedded words she had long been trying to say, but never had she seen such a disagreeable look on Mr Fothergill's face.

'Married? Married?' he bellowed. 'I didn't know that someone had asked for your hand. Why was I not consulted in this matter? I've been your guardian now for five years, responsible for your well-being. Have I not taught you to read and write and appreciate the finer things in life? Am I to be ignored now that you are making the biggest decision of your life? Who is this blackguard?'

'No, no, sir. There's no such person yet. Nor will there be until he has spoken to you first. It is merely a desire I have. A desire I can't explain.'

Regretting his outburst he suddenly began to see Lizzie in a different light. For five years he had taken Lizzie for granted, thinking she would always be there to look after him. Unnoticed, she had grown into a fine young lady. He pulled a chair out from the kitchen table and sat down ready to talk further. She took a seat next to him and spoke to him as convincingly as she could.

'I know, sir, that you are anxious to employ a butler. I remember you saying that a butler would be a companion for you and there was someone you had in mind. Well,' she said, shuffling her chair nearer to him, 'if I were to marry and live with my husband there would be room then for your someone to move in here.'

'If this is what you wish then we must find you a suitable husband,' the headmaster said, thinking how convenient it would be to have his gentleman friend from Harrogate living with him in the guise of butler. There would be no need to make so many long, arduous journeys into town and he could spend so much more time in his comfortable home. There would be time to write and paint, or even travel abroad together with his companion to look for exotic plants. He would miss Lizzie, though, she was so efficient and had looked after him well.

*

Reuben arrived later that evening. After a short discussion with Mr Fothergill about the legal matters concerning Reuben's inheritance of North Fell, the subject of finding a wife was approached. Determined that Reuben's matrimonial problem should be turned to his own advantage, Mr Fothergill came straight to the point.

'I've found you a young lady who I'm sure would be willing to be your wife.'

'Oh, yes a wife. I need a wife,' Reuben said as if marriage was an unwelcome condition, a prospect he did not relish but had to suffer in order to inherit the farmstead.

'Yes. I think Lizzie would make an excellent wife for you.'

'Lizzie? Your Lizzie?'

'Yes. I can't think of anyone better.'

'But she's just a young lass. Oh no, Mr Fothergill, it wouldn't be proper for a man of my age to marry such a young girl.'

'Have you looked at her lately? She is eighteen years old now, and a very comely young lady she is too. She would make the perfect wife for you.'

'But the work on the farm will be much too hard for her. I will need all the help a wife can give me. No, Lizzie is not the right one. I need someone hardened to the outdoor life.'

'She's not afraid of hard work. She's very capable, a good cook, neat and tidy. I can vouch that she would be very faithful and loyal. I'll send for her and then leave the room on a pretence so you can talk. I'm sure you'll be pleasantly surprised. Mark my word, Reuben, you will not find anyone better in such a short time.'

Lizzie, who was waiting in the kitchen and hoping that her renewed scheming was going to plan, was ready when the servants' bell rang, summoning her to the parlour. Not wanting to appear too eager she waited a little while, then knocked on the parlour door and entered.

'Lizzie, come in,' Mr Fothergill said, pulling a chair up to the desk for her and dipping the quill in the ink before handing it to her.

'Will you make a list of the provisions we're in need of while I still have them on my mind? I am busy and likely to forget.'

'Good evening, Mr Webster,' Lizzie said alluringly as she pushed past him. She went to the desk, took the white feather quill from Mr Fothergill, and began to write, the nib scratching across the paper as he dictated.

'I'm not sure about the brandy and wine. The rector emptied a decanter on his last visit.' he said, pointing a finger into the air as if to appear thoughtful. 'I'll go to the cellar and check how many we need. It may take a while.'

He nodded with encouragement towards Reuben as he left the room.

Reuben watched Lizzie gliding the pen confidently across the paper and was impressed by the fact that she could read and write, a mystery he had never mastered to any satisfaction, and thought she must be very clever. He thought she didn't look strong enough for the hard work that was ahead at North Fell, but on the other hand, that slice of bacon she had given him had tasted delicious. Maybe Mr Fothergill was right, possibly it could be workable and she would not make such a bad wife after all. The sooner he was married the sooner he would have his farm, and he was anxious to get started on all the work there was to be done up there. He made his mind up instantly and blurted out, 'Lizzie, will you marry me?'

'Yes,' she said emphatically and without hesitation, surprising Reuben by her quick answer.

'Oh, right then, that's settled. Right. I'll be off then,' he said and made a hasty departure, leaving any arrangements for the wedding and their life together unplanned.

Chapter 4

Sunday morning brought rare tranquillity to Little Dindley village; the silence broken only by the ringing of the church bell. The hammer hitting cracked metal, weakened by a flawed casting, emitted a distorted clank which resounded mournfully and echoed down the valley. Punctual as always the rector pulled monotonously on the bell rope, calling his flock to prayer. The church door, open wide, demanded the presence of his parishioners. In their entirety they assembled. Dressed in their finery and nodding salutations, they took their places in pews appointed according to rank and status. The family from the manor, known locally as the big house, sat in the front under the pulpit and their servants out of sight at the back. Reuben and Lizzie, assigned to the back of the church, waited to be called upon. Lizzie, very excited, wriggled on the seat, a big smile on her face. She was nearly there. Nearly Reuben's wife.

With his flock finally gathered and the first hymn sung, the Reverend Augustus Sewell took his position in the pulpit and started his sermon. His black robe squarely covered his knee breeches and emphasised his spindly stocking-clad legs. His sunken eyes glared out from a wild mane of grey hair and emphatic arm waving highlighted the important words and caused the starched white ruff round his neck to roll up and down. The sermon seemed to go on forever. He thumped his fist down heavily and his sudden loud outcry woke, with a jolt, those who dared to sleep. The evils of Hell and damnation, and the threat of eternal punishment which would accompany those who did evil brought shocked gasps from the faint-hearted members of the congregation who just wanted the sermon over and done with. They were impatient for the more entertaining part of the service to start, and which they had all come to witness.

An 'amen' ended the sermon and the rector made his way to the front of the altar, his willowy finger beckoning the matrimonial couple forward. Conversations stopped in mid-sentence and heads turned to the back of the church.

Reuben hesitated. *What am I doing?* he thought, *Taking on this young girl, for better or worse, for the rest of my life.* This was not what he wanted, but a forceful push from Lizzie left him flustered and unwittingly walking up the aisle beside her. The hushed congregation sat in anticipation to witness this extraordinary wedding.

'On this first Sunday in August in your presence, I announce the marriage to take place in this church of Reuben Webster to Elizabeth Jane Palmer, both of this parish. Would the appointed witnesses please step forward?'

Mr Fothergill rose from his seat midway down the congregation, pulled satisfactorily on his waistcoat, and offered his arm to Annie Webster, Reuben's sister, before accompanying her to stand at the altar beside the couple.

The stern-faced rector cleared his throat and, looking over the top of his pince-nez spectacles, asked severely, 'Do you, Reuben Webster, take Elizabeth Jane Palmer to be your lawful wedded wife?'

Reuben, a tall man and eleven years older than Lizzie, pulled his shoulders back and stood to his full height. 'Aye, I do,' he said.

'Do you, Elizabeth Jane Palmer, take Reuben Webster to be your lawful wedded husband?'

There was no answer. Bowing his head intently towards her, the rector waited for an answer. He repeated the question. Lizzie looked up into his eyes, but all she could see was an image of him bouncing up and down on his pony. She put her hand tightly over her mouth to stifle the overwhelming urge to giggle; her shoulders shaking with the restraint. Trying so hard but fuelled by the excitement of the ceremony she was unable to hold back any longer and burst into helpless laughter.

'Elizabeth, you must take your vows very seriously or we cannot continue with this wedding,' the rector said piously, his austere attitude inflaming the situation even more.

Reuben, trying to calm the dilemma, clenched his teeth and nudged her astutely with his elbow, but his effort was to no avail; she just could not stop laughing.

'Be'ave Lizzie,' he scolded in a loud whisper from the corner of his mouth.

A mixture of amusement and disbelief swept through the congregation, and they chatted and sniggered behind cupped hands. Finding the laughter infectious, their scorn quickly turned into unruly laughter, adding to Lizzie's frivolous behaviour. The rector had never witnessed such blasphemy and felt quite powerless as to how to restore solemnity back to his church. Becoming exasperated and tired of waiting for Lizzie to compose herself and give her answer, he looked up to the heavens for celestial guidance. He closed the big, heavy prayer book he was holding with an almighty slam which echoed round the nave like a shot from a gun, bringing a sudden halt to the joviality. His spectacles fell from the end of his long nose as he bent forward, his face red with anger, and looked straight into Lizzie's eyes.

'I will take it, Lizzie, seeing as you are still stood here, that your answer is yes,' he said.

Realising she must quickly calm down or her scheming over the past weeks was once again going to end in disaster, Lizzie stood with her head bowed. She silently nodded her head. The rector, with a sigh of hopelessness and no wish for the uproar to restart, quickly brought the ceremony to a close, announcing, 'Let there be no more hilarity. Reuben and Elizabeth, you are now married in the eyes of God. I now pronounce you husband and wife. May God in his mercy bless you both. Now, be off with you.'

Reuben grabbed Lizzie's sleeve. Thoroughly embarrassed, he

walked as quickly as possible through the giggling congregation and headed for the door, dragging her behind him. In the churchyard he spun her round to face him.

'Let go, you're hurting my arm.'

'How could you humiliate me like that? You will have to conduct yourself better in future if you are to be my wife.'

The reprimand fell on deaf ears; she could not understand that she had done anything wrong. All Lizzie wanted now was to see the cottage; her new home. She pulled her arm free, let her shawl fall from her head, held it tight with one hand, picked up her skirt with the other, and shouted, 'Race you to the cottage,' as she set off full pace down the churchyard path, leaving Reuben shaking his head in disbelief.

What have I done? he thought.

Chapter 5

Lizzie raced on ahead. She ran as fast as her legs would carry her with a picture in her mind of the cottage where she and Reuben were to live. Behind her, Reuben dawdled along the drovers' road at his own speed, still angry with her for her unforgivable outburst of laughter in the church. It was not her behaviour which had embarrassed him, it was the fact that it had been witnessed by the whole village and would be the topic of gossip for a long time.

Before he crossed the packhorse bridge, he stopped to look at the forge, the most outlying building in the village. The adjoining blacksmith's cottage was where, twenty eight years ago, he had been born. He was the second son of blacksmith John Webster. His father, who had died eight years previously, had failed to make a will and the eldest son, Jack Webster, had taken it upon himself to take possession of all the property and the blacksmith business for himself.

'I'm master 'ere now,' Jack had told Reuben. 'There's not enough work to feed me, m' wife and you an' all. You'll have to seek your own work someplace else.'

This left Reuben unexpectedly without work and having to frequent hiring fairs in the nearby towns. He had stood for hours, degraded, while ruthless employers looked him up and down while they decided whether or not to give him a chance. The only offer he had received had been to work at the big house for the squire who was looking to hire able-bodied men. He would also be expected to join the militia when called upon. He took it, thinking not only was it work but it would be somewhere to live as well. He also considered the area too remote for him to ever be called up by the army.

Lizzie had by now crossed the packhorse bridge, slowing down and picking her footholds carefully on the cobble-stoned incline. She turned and waved excitedly at Reuben, 'Come on, I'm winning,' he heard her shout before she ran off up the steep hill of North Fell.

Reuben leant on the gate of the smithy's paddock. A heavy horse, left to graze in the paddock and ready to be the first shoeing of the Monday morning queue, chinked a loose shoe as it scraped its foot on the hard sun-baked ground. Reuben clicked his tongue in the side of his mouth. The big horse immediately picked up its head, plodded obediently towards him, and nuzzled its snorting nostrils up to Reuben's chest expecting to be fed a titbit.

'I've got nought for you, old girl,' he said, stroking the animal's neck and running his rough calloused hands down the horse's leg to feel the firm muscles. 'My, you're a beauty. I'll own the likes of you one day.'

The horse, feeling the familiar hand and knowing the routine, lifted the foot with the loose shoe.

'No, that's not my job any more,' he said, smacking its big rump and nostalgically thinking of the past. His only ambition in life had been to take over from his father as blacksmith of Dindley. There had been many bitter arguments between the two brothers since the death of their father, especially during the times when Reuben could not find work or anywhere to live. Arguments which had still not been resolved.

Reuben was jolted out of his reminiscence by the noise of people coming out of the church and the village coming back to life. The main topic of gossip by the busybodies today would be his quick marriage to young Lizzie, and he had no intention of explaining his actions. He disappeared into the forge while Jack was not there to collect some tools and various provisions he thought would be useful on his farm.

*

Still giggling, Lizzie raced on but was getting out of breath. She tried to keep up her speed but the hill was steep and brambles had encroached on to the rough track, making it difficult to find a way through. At one point a big branch, fallen from a gnarled old oak tree, lay across the path. It was much too heavy for her to lift and she had to step to one side down into a ditch to get past it. She had half-run, half-walked the two miles from the church, and soon she would be there at her new home. She romanced with the idea of filling the cottage with beautiful things and dancing in and out of all the rooms. This was the start of her new life. At last her desire for happiness would be accomplished. She had lost sight of Reuben and planned to find a place in the cottage to hide and jump out to surprise him when he arrived.

Turning the last corner, the cottage was there in front of her. She brought her hands together as if her prayers had been answered; but it was not prayer that her hands were expressing, it was horror. Never had she seen such a ramshackle building.

This can't be it. I must have the wrong place. Did I take a wrong turn? she thought. She could not have done as there were no turnings to take, just one long, steep lane and there, sure enough, was the name on the rickety old gate: Townsend Cottage.

The door hung perilously on one rusty hinge and grated noisily when she tried to open it. Giving it a big push she sent it swinging backwards into the room. There were just two small windows, shuttered and letting in no light, making the room especially dim to Lizzie's eyes as she came in from the bright sunlight.

The stone-flagged floor was strewn with decaying foliage and dried leaves which crunched like frozen snow as she walked on them. She did not see the overturned chair lying in the middle of the floor and fell across it, landing in a pile of ash which had spread out from the open hearth. A mouse scurried across her feet and disappeared into the safety of a pile of debris. Disturbed dust danced in the shaft of light which shone into a corner of the room from the open door.

She scrambled to her feet, dusting herself down and cursing silently to herself. She struggled to open one of the shutters but age had rendered the iron fittings immoveable. Losing her temper she thumped aggressively at the shutter with both fists, cursing out loud and sure that the Devil himself had brought her to this ungodly place. Splinters of wood cut deep into her hands. With teeth clenched she gave one sharp pull and the shutter broke away from the wall and disintegrated into powdery pieces as it crashed in a cloud of dust on the floor.

Lifting the lid from an iron cooking pot sitting in the cinders, she saw mouldy remains of a meal. She reeled backwards as the stale musty smell made her sneeze. Dirty crockery had been left on a table. Rodent droppings were evidence that any food which might have been there had been eaten. In an alcove at the side of the hearth a limply draped curtain hid a small bed. She tweaked the feather mattress and a mouse jumped out and ran into the corner of the room to join the other one in the pile of debris.

There was a rustic ladder leading vertically up to a loft. Holding on tightly she ventured on to the first rung then slowly on to the second and third until her eyes were level with the dusty wooden floor above. A bed was pushed against the chimney stack and she could see a cracked chamber pot beneath it. She did not feel very safe on the ladder and was too frightened to climb any higher. Without looking down she put one foot out and felt for the rung below but could not find it. She glanced down to find the step but became dizzy and thought she might fall. She waited for a while then tried again. It was no good, she could neither go up nor climb down.

She looked longingly at the chamber pot. Red and yellow roses were painted on the side and matched a jug and basin on top of a washstand which was pushed under the beams of the low, sloping roof. Her knuckles were turning white from holding on so tightly and she desperately needed to use that chamber pot.

'Reuben,' she shouted with anguish. She pursed her lips and drew in her breath. 'Oooh, Reuben, where are you?'

*

Reuben was still inside the forge selecting implements he would need. He piled them on to an old two-wheeled handcart which had been propped up in a corner unused for many years. Suddenly a shout from behind made him swing round.

'What the blazes do you think you're up to?' Jack had arrived home from church just a little too soon for Reuben's liking. Reuben, not wanting an argument, did not answer but kept on loading the cart.

'Where the hell d'ya think you're taking all that lot?' Jack asked, storming round the other side of the cart, then started to unload it and drop things to the floor.

Reuben still did not speak. He gave Jack one almighty push, quickly picked up the dropped items, put them back on the cart, then hurriedly left, dragging the cart behind him and leaving Jack thoroughly incensed.

The overladen cart bumped across the cobbles of the packhorse bridge and rattled and groaned up the steep rough track to North Fell. Reuben tried pushing then pulling, undecided as to which was the easiest way to handle it. The hot midday sun was unrelenting and the sight of the heavy branch blocking the path did nothing to ease his already ruffled temper. He struggled for some time before he was able to move it safely off the path then collected some of the deadwood on to the cart for the cottage fire.

Even above the clatter of the iron-rimmed wheels Reuben could hear Lizzie shouting. The pitch of her cries were near hysteria as she clung paralysed to the vertical loft ladder.

'Stop being so giddy,' Reuben shouted through the open cottage door. 'Calm yourself, child. I haven't time to play your games, there's work to be done.' He continued on round to the backyard to find a place to store the tools and handcart. He eventually made his entrance through the back door and pottered about in the scullery before he noticed Lizzie still halfway up the ladder.

'Good lass, have you been preparing the bed? We'll be toil-worn before this day is done and be well glad of somewhere ready to rest.'

'No, I have not been preparing the bed, now help me down from here.'

When Reuben looked at her he saw tears running down her face.

'Whatever's the matter now? First you can't stop laughing and make a right spectacle of yourself in the church. Now you're bawling.'

'The Lord is punishing me. He's stuck me to the spot so that I cannot move. I've been on this ladder so long I thought I was here for ever. Where have you been?'

'Come on, Mrs Webster,' he said, putting his big hands round her tiny waist and lifting her down. She wanted to fling her arms around him and kiss him but there was no time. Distressed, Lizzie dashed straight through the open scullery door into the backyard to find the privy. Down the garden path, round the pigsty, she found it. A tumbledown wooden lean-to with a single seat over a bucket. A gruesome smelly place. She kicked the door hard to scare any rats which might be lurking inside but she was so desperate she did not have time to wait for them to run away.

Chapter 6

When Lizzie returned to the room, she could hear Reuben moving about above in the open sleeping loft. If she stood at the opposite side of the room she could just see him through the cracks in the old, worn-out floorboards. He was undressing and taking off the silk waistcoat which Mr Fothergill had given him to wear at the wedding. Mr Fothergill was a short, fat man, but despite his portly figure was a flamboyant dresser and had a collection of waistcoats. The one he had given to Reuben was ill-fitting for such a tall man and the glossy material had looked ostentatious against his coarse woollen Sunday breeches, but had served as a vain attempt to announce his new status of farmer. He was intrigued how the light played tricks on the material and made the silk change colour. He stroked the soft fabric with the back of his hand before carefully folding it and hanging it over the end of the bed. His shirt, made of bleached shoddy – a much inferior cloth – was hastily removed and thrown on the bed.

He then began to unbuckle his trouser belt and Lizzie, although anxious of the outcome, peeped inquisitively. Without taking her gaze from him she stepped quietly sideways to get a better view but bumped clumsily into the table, sending the dirty plates rolling and clattering on the floor among the litter.

'Lizzie, is that you?' he shouted.

'Yes.'

'Come up here and get that dress off,' he ordered, unnerving Lizzie who was horrified at the thought of him taking her so soon. She was not quite sure what he would do to her, it was all a mystery, but she had no intention of finding out so early in the day. She aimed to delay the ordeal, whatever it involved, as long as she could.

'I'm busy. Really busy,' she shouted back, desperately looking for something to occupy herself with. She picked the plates up from the floor and walked round with them as if she were looking for somewhere to clean them and put them away.

'Get that dress off,' he repeated as he descended the ladder, sending Lizzie scurrying into a corner like a startled animal.

'I must look away until you are fully dressed,' she said, covering her eyes with her hand.

'Damn it, girl, I am fully dressed. Look I've just changed into m'old clothes. There's work waiting to be done this day. You get this place cleaned up while I see what's outside. Now get that dress off and put it away safe before you spoil it. It'll be a long while before you get another.'

With all expectations of the fine clothes she had hoped for gone she stood, disheartened, turning round and round looking at the overwhelming mess. She did not know where to start.

'I can't live here in this midden. I want to go back to Mr Fothergill's house.'

'You know you can't do that. Mrs Dawson is there doing your job until the butler arrives. This is your home now.'

'I don't like it here. You don't expect me to live here, do you? It's dirty and horrid.'

'Well clean it. You're not feared of a bit of dust are you? I'm going up on the fell to look at the state of the stone walls. I'll need some good holding pens if I'm to bring them sheep down off the moor for shearing. Should have been done last month. I want to see this place clean when I get back. Now get changed out of that dress and put it away.'

'I can't. I didn't bring any clothes with me. All my things are still at the nice, clean house.'

'Well, take the cart and go get 'em. Be quick and don't stand gossiping. There's much to be done before it gets dark.'

She was very upset by his sudden aggression and sulked like a spoilt child as she tried to control the unwieldy handcart she pushed the two miles to Mr Fothergill's house.

*

Mrs Dawson, a buxom woman expecting her sixth child, greeted her at the back door.

'Hello m'dear. Well, ye gods and little fishes, you look a right one all dressed up in your wedding dress and pushing that dirty old barra'.'

Irritated further, Lizzie stamped her foot and sent the handcart crashing into the garden wall.

'Well, there's a fine to-do,' said Mrs Dawson. 'Now look what you've done. One of the wheels is broken.'

'I don't care. I've come back home.'

'Temper, temper. Has he upset you already?'

'Oh, Mrs Dawson, I've seen rats as big as dogs, six of 'em running about in that house of his.'

'Come in and tell me all about it and let me have a look at this lovely dress. I think it's the prettiest dress I've ever seen.'

Given the chance to show off, Lizzie soon forgot her troubles. She held out the skirt of the linen dress with both hands to reveal the full extent of the embroidered hem. She danced around the big kitchen like the belle of the ball.

'Slow down, you'll make yourself dizzy. What a lovely colour. It's the gold of a cornfield ready to harvest. Here, let me feel. It's so soft,' said Mrs Dawson, rubbing the material against her cheek.

'Annie gave it me. The lace collar came all the way from Nottingham she told me.'

'Annie? Reuben's sister?'

'Aye.'

'Mistress Prim, I call her,' said Mrs Dawson.

'Aye,' laughed Lizzie. 'I call her Mistress Strait-Lace.'

'Well, you're the honoured one. I've never known her to give the time of day.'

'She said that if I was to be a Webster I'd better smarten myself up and look like one.'

'That sounds just like 'er. Rides around in that pony and trap, never walks anywhere. Them Websters always did think they were better than anyone else in the village, but they'll get their comeuppance one day, mark my word. Well, child, you've made your bed and now you must lie on it. Off you go back up there.'

'Nightmares will fill my nights if I have to sleep up there. I'd rather sleep with the Devil in the graveyard.'

'May the blessed Lord deliver us all from evil,' blasphemed Mrs Dawson.

'I'm not going back there,' Lizzie said defiantly.

'You can't sleep here, my dear, the butler arrives tonight with all his goods and chattels. He's travelling on the mail coach and Mr Fothergill has gone to Ripon to collect him. I've prepared your old room for him but I don't suppose he'll abide in there for long with no bedfellow. Rum goings on if you ask me.'

'What do you mean?'

'You'll find out when you're older, my girl.'

'When will that be? Everyone treats me like a child. I'm a married woman now.'

'Ah, well then, you'll know all about it now.'

'What do you mean? Know all about what?'

'What Reuben will want. Have you been in his bed yet?'

'No, though he cannot wait to rid me of my dress. I'm a little afraid of him.'

'And you with no mother to comfort you or sister to talk to,' sympathised Mrs Dawson, but she realised it was not really her place to teach this young girl the ways of the world. Goodness knew why nobody had told her what to expect.

'I just want to know what he'll do to me,' said Lizzie, hoping for at least a little information.

'You'll find out. You just lie back and keep still while he does what he has to do. Now you get along and hurry back to that husband of yours. I'll take the cart to the forge, get Jack to mend it, and I'll bring it up to Townsend Cottage with all your things tomorrow.'

Mrs Dawson, well known for ferreting about in other peoples' affairs, saw this as an ideal opportunity to view the cottage and be predominant with the latest gossip. Even though her legs were swollen with the dropsy and she was heavily pregnant, it would not stop her getting there.

It was very late when Reuben got back to the cottage. He stood outside for a while watching bats zigzagging about, satisfied so far with his inheritance. He found Lizzie curled up on the little bed in the fireside alcove. No cleaning had been done and he despaired that it ever would. He was pleased with his farm and had enjoyed walking on the moors among his sheep, but he did not have the wife he had expected. She was still wearing her wedding dress and had not changed as he had asked. He thought how beautiful she looked asleep, but to him she was still very young and it would not be right to impose himself upon her.

Her long black curls fell across her face and Reuben gently brushed them back. Lizzie lay quite still and kept her eyes closed until he had climbed the stair ladder and she had heard him get in to the big bed. When she eventually heard him snoring she breathed a sigh of relief but lay awake for a long time wondering why she had not asked Mr Fothergill for time from her duties to see the house before she married. She had been allowed one day off a month but had never requested it as she had no friends or family to visit and, over the years, the day had become obsolete. Changing her mind now was not an option and she fell asleep determined to make the best of this terrible mistake she had made.

Chapter 7

The sweltering heat in the forge soon built up as Jack Webster pumped the bellows to bring a satisfying glow to the fire. The forge in winter was a good place to work; the warmest place in the village. Men would congregate round the furnace to keep warm while waiting for the inn to open or just for conversation's sake, but on this hot Monday morning in early August the heat was enough to test the patience of even the most saintly. Cartwheels, hoops, ironwork and harnesses littered the walls and floor and all manner of tools, metal patterns and pokers hung from low beams like stalactites. Two horses, tethered to rings in the walls, snorted noisily as the smoke invaded their nostrils. The rank smell of their hot bodies wafted through the workshop.

Jack Webster, unlike his brother Reuben, was a big, muscular man, barrel-chested with his face hidden behind an unkempt beard extending into his nose and ears. A thick leather split-apron tied with rope round his big girth covered most of his body from his breast to below his knees. He was an austere man who liked to quench his thirst a little too often in the inn and could stand his ground in any fist fight or argument.

A full day's work waited for the blacksmith and he was eager to get started. Before working on the tethered horses, his first job this morning was to shoe the heavy horse which had been in the paddock overnight. Bobby Saunders sat on the wall waiting to lead it up from the paddock and fasten it to the wall outside the forge, the first of a few errands which would earn him a copper or two. Jack Webster's enthusiasm was slowing down by the time he got to shoeing all four feet of a dales pony, he was ready for the ale that would be waiting for him at the inn.

Bobby took the pony and the two horses to the paddock to graze and wait for collection, but only when payment had been made by their owners. He then led the heavy horse some distance away to the hayfields where work was held up until its arrival.

About midday the heat had become overpowering so Jack let the fire die down and turned his hand to finishing a wooden coffin he had made for a young woman who had died in childbirth. It was slightly wider at one side to allow the baby, who had only lived for an hour, to lie beside her. He was busy fitting the metal handles and hinges when he heard hooves scraping on the cobbles outside the forge door. When he looked up the sun was directly in his eyes. All he could see was the silhouette of a horseman framed by the opening of the wide forge door, the sunlight behind the rider forming a halo round his top hat.

'What can I do for you?' Jack shouted.

'Would you be Jack Webster, son of John Webster?' the rider asked without alighting from his horse.

'Aye, that's me. Blacksmith of this village. You a stranger in these parts then?' asked Jack, putting down his tools and strolling towards the door, puffing out his chest and mopping the sweat from his brow with a well-used rag.

'Good morning to you on this fine day, Mr Webster.'

Jack touched his forelock and nodded acknowledgement to the finely dressed man. He walked round the horse, patting its rump and admiring the expensive saddle. A design he had not seen before.

'That's a mighty fine horse you have there, sir. I've let the fire down but if it's shoes you're after I can soon build it up again.'

'No, that's not what I'm here for. My horse is adequately taken care of elsewhere.'

'What business do you have with me then?' asked Jack.

'Are you John Webster, known as Jack, son of John Webster, blacksmith, deceased?'

'Aye I am. I already said so.'

The horseman leaned down over the side of his horse and proffered his hand to Jack who, thinking he might get some high society business from this man, wiped his dirty hand down the side of his breeches and unwittingly stretched his arm up to shake. Before their hands made contact, a ribboned scroll was quickly and firmly placed into Jack's hand.

'I am here to inform you that an agreement has been prepared between you and the trustees of the late Widow Learoyd's estate for collection of unpaid rent.'

'Unpaid rent? You've got the wrong man, good sir. I owe nothing and pay rent to no person.' said Jack with a burst of his usual raucous laughter and raising the scroll in the air in an attempt to give it back.

'I can assure you it is for you, Mr Webster. The sum of one hundred pounds is owing.'

'One hundred pounds? That's a handsome sum. I've never seen one hundred pounds in my life.'

'You will find full details of the assessment in the rent roll I have just given you.'

'One hundred pounds? Sir, there must be a mistake. Rent? What for?' gasped Jack, looking at the ribboned scroll in his hand and again offered it back.

'Your rent, Mr Webster, for the substantial property you use here. The sum includes the meadows, the paddock and the orchards, the cottage and also commercial use of the forge. Considering you have had the property for eight years without payment, the Learoyds have been more than generous in their valuation.'

'To hell with the Learoyds. I'm damned if I'll pay rent to them or anyone else.'

Jack tried to grab the horse's reins, once again attempting to give the scroll back to the horseman, but the rider quickly pulled his horse's head round and turned to leave.

'The payment will become due in total on Michaelmas Day. Good day, Mr Webster.' He pressed his top hat to secure it tightly on his head, dug his heels into the horse's flanks, and rode away at a brisk pace, leaving the bewildered blacksmith holding the scroll.

Chapter 8

Mrs Dawson made her way up the hill to North Fell; the track twisting and turning up the steep-sided valley. She puffed and cursed as she trudged along the rough ground, dragging the cart containing Lizzie's belongings behind her, harnessed between the handles like a brood mare. The slope was proving to be too much for a woman in her condition, but her curiosity fed her determination to continue. Lizzie, anxious to get her belongings, had been watching from the cottage window for almost an hour. The window was in a position which gave a good view of the distant valley and most of the Dindley village. She could see that the river, usually fast-flowing and deep, was very low due to the hot weather and lack of rain. As soon as she saw Mrs Dawson approaching, she ran down the lane to meet her.

'Thank heavens,' said Mrs Dawson, stopping to get her breath back. 'Help me pull this blasted thing, I'm done in. What do you want all these heavy books for anyway?'

'I like reading books. I find them interesting and you can learn such a lot from them.'

'They're the work of the Devil if you ask me. All this learning ain't for the likes of you and me. It'll rot your brain.'

'Nonsense, Mrs Dawson. I'm going to be someone important one day.'

'Oh aye,' scoffed Mrs Dawson. 'I doubt it very much but you can live in hope, I suppose.'

'You wait and see if I'm not,' bragged Lizzie, grabbing one of the handles and helping to pull the damaged handcart. She giggled as the bent wheel bumped and wobbled over the stony ground sending the cart swerving in all directions. Everything she owned was in this little cart, but she was determined to improve on all that in the future.

'I thought you were going to get the cart mended,' said Lizzie.

'I asked Jack but he wouldn't. I've tied it up as best I could. Might just make it up there as far as the cottage.'

Lizzie didn't take much notice, she was having too much fun trying to steer it and planning where she would put her things in the cottage. The rest of the way did not take long with the two of them pulling, and they were soon at the rickety cottage door.

'Come in, come in,' Lizzie shouted excitedly as she ran in and out unloading the contents of the cart.

'Phew. Have you got a chair?' asked Mrs Dawson, her hands soothing her arched back. 'This bairn is weighing heavy. I'll be glad when it's born.'

Lizzie picked the chair up from where it still lay upturned on the floor and blew some dust from the seat. Mrs Dawson flopped down on to it with a thud, making a cloud of the remaining dust. She coughed and wafted her hand in front of her face to clear the air.

'I tell Mr Dawson we can't find food for another one but he says they all bring their love with 'em. Well he would, wouldn't he? As long as he gets his way, he doesn't care.'

Mr Dawson, just as slender as his wife was fat, owned a small piece of land. He had been a hard worker and his fields had been just enough to bring in sufficient income to support his ever growing young family. A carefree man who loved all his children equally, he was now unable to work his land. A year ago he had an accident while harnessing his horse to the plough. He had become trapped in the shafts and the horse had trampled him. A very badly broken leg, despite treatment and loving care by his wife, did not repair properly and meant that Mr Dawson had been unable to continue working. A small income from leasing the land did not bring enough money in and now things were looking bleak. It would be another year before the eldest child was thirteen and old enough to earn a wage, so Mrs Dawson earned what she could by doing casual work around the village.

Her nose turned up as she looked round the cottage, her head rising and falling, remembering points that would make good gossip back in the village. She liked being the centre of attention by being first with snippets she could enthuse about. She chatted on from one subject to another of little interest to Lizzie, almost forgetting her latest news.

'There was a stranger at the forge,' she suddenly remembered.

'Where shall I put these?' said Lizzie, wandering around with an armful of books.

'Real toff he was,' said Mrs Dawson.

'I think I'll have to put the best books under my bed.'

'Are you listening to me? '

'Yes. Go on.'

'They were quarrelling.'

'Who was?' asked Lizzie'

'The man at Jack Webster's place. Jack was having a right argument with him. Shouting and pushing each other about. Jack tried to pull him off his horse.'

'He argues with everyone, Jack Webster does. He means no harm,' said Lizzie.

'And that wife of his is no better either,' said Mrs Dawson. 'She was there with her arms folded nodding in agreement every time Jack said something.'

'What was the argument about?'

'Don't rightly know but Jack was telling him to get off his land. When the stranger rode off I pointed to the barra', explained it was Reuben's and asked would he mend it. He just shouted, "Tell Reuben to go to hell". Voice like thunder he had. There was no need to speak to me like that, I told him but he just pushed Mrs Webster into the house and disappeared inside after her.'

Lizzie showed little interest, she was more concerned about her belongings. There were no shelves for her books, no pegs for her clothes, nor cupboards for the housewares she had acquired, *borrowed* she called it, from Mr Fothergill's kitchen.

'Bit of a mess in here, like you said. But nothing that can't be put to rights. I'll stay awhile and help you if you like. We'll need some hot water. Is there a set pot in the scullery?'

'Yes, but there's a weaving loom in there taking up most of the space, you'll have to squeeze passed it.'

'You mean you will, my girl, not me,' said Mrs Dawson from the confines of the chair. 'Now find some kindling and get some water boiling in that pot. All this dried bracken on the floor will do as kindling to light the fire.'

The set pot was built into the wall and could hold a substantial amount of water; it took Lizzie a few journeys to the brook to fetch enough to fill it. The grate underneath soon had a good fire burning and it did not take long to heat the water to the required temperature.

The day passed quickly as the two women sang happily while they swept, scrubbed and washed nearly everything in the cottage. The bedding, which had been laundered and draped over bushes to dry in the sun, was placed back on the beds, Mrs Dawson having to climb the loft ladder to see to the big bed while Lizzie made the excuse that her preference was to fetch water from the nearby beck.

Mrs Dawson had prepared food and was giving a final stir to a large cook pot simmering on the kitchen fire when Reuben returned. From the open door he saw the fat figure leaning over the pot like a witch at her cauldron. He was hot and tired, and after a hard day's work repairing dry stone walls and sheep pens on the edge of the moor he had no desire to be greeted with the likes of her.

'Where's Lizzie?' he asked indignantly.

'Hello, Mr Webster. She's just there in the scullery,' she replied, smiling and waiting for compliments on the transformed state of the cottage.

'Lizzie,' he shouted with anger in his voice, 'get yourself in here.'

Lizzie entered the room from the scullery, drying her wet hands on the side of her pinafore. 'Hello Reuben, look at . . .'

'What's she doing here?' Reuben asked, rudely pointing a finger at Mrs Dawson.

'Mrs Dawson has very kindly been here all day helping me. Look how lovely and tidy everything is.'

'Get gone, woman, out of my house,' he said, stepping aside and holding the door wide open, gesturing to Mrs Dawson. 'This is Lizzie's work not yours. Be on your way and see to your own.'

'Reuben, hold your tongue,' interrupted Lizzie. 'You must not turn her out of doors without any thanks until you know all that she's done and the great help she's been to me.'

'Mrs Dawson, leave my house,' he said, ignoring Lizzie, 'and don't come back unless I invite you.'

'For heaven's sake, Reuben, don't be so harsh,' said Lizzie.

'Don't argue with me, child.'

Lizzie could not believe what she was hearing. She came from a family home where friends had always been welcome and felt belittled at once again being called a child.

'I'm not a child,' she protested, but Reuben was not listening and continued to argue with Mrs Dawson.

'Well, I never. In all my years I've not been told to leave somebody's home,' said Mrs Dawson. 'If that's all the thanks I get, I swear on the cross I will never enter this house again.'

'Good, that'll suit me fine,' said Reuben.

'May God forgive you your temper, Mr Webster,' said Mrs Dawson

Reuben slammed the door after her, almost catching her foot. She ran from the cottage down the garden path as fast as her rotund body would allow. Stopping at the gate with her hands on her hips, humiliated, she stared back at the closed door in disbelief. Lizzie had run to the small alcove bed and buried her head in the mattress to hide the tears welling up in her eyes. She knew she had to start standing up to this man, but she was so angry at Reuben's behaviour that she could not help being tearful.

'I hate you,' she shouted, lifting her head long enough for Reuben to hear her anguish.

'I know better than you how she goes round the village tittle-tattling about other peoples' affairs. What she can't find out she makes up, spreading stories which aren't true. What have you been telling her?'

'Nothing.'

'She's been here all day and you've told her nothing? What did you talk about?'

'I think you're losing your reason. Am I not to entertain my friends here when you are out all day leaving me here alone?'

'Entertain? Entertain? You didn't marry the squire. You married a poor shepherd and your days will be filled with work, not entertaining.'

'And when my work is done, what then?' she asked sarcastically.

'Don't be so disrespectful. I will have no one in my house and you will obey my wishes.'

'No one? asked Lizzie. 'Not even your prim and proper sister Annie, or your uncouth brother Jack?'

'Especially not my brother Jack.'

Chapter 9

The forge was a well-equipped building and the adjoining cottage, having three bedrooms, was a sizeable, comfortable family home. It was a corner building positioned where the drovers' road forked into two; one road led to Ripon and the other was a track crossing the humpbacked packhorse bridge leading up the steep valley side to North Fell.

In his lifetime John Webster, Reuben's father, had been a hardworking, honest man and, over the years, his labours had established a profitable blacksmith business. As a skilled craftsman he had always been ready to turn his hand to any other job that needed doing in the village such as laying out the bodies of the dead and coffin making; soldering pots, pans and candlesticks; or any repair required for the smooth running of households.

A caring man, he had been well respected in the area for his integrity and involvement in the parish council. Born in Dindley, as were his parents, he had married his childhood friend, Charlotte, who had also been born in the village. They'd had a good life, not extravagant because John and his money were not easily parted, but comfortable enough.

Charlotte happily bore him five children but only three survived into adulthood. Their firstborn, a son, took John's name but, to save any confusion, became known as Jack Webster. Unlike his father, he grew to be a hard loutish man with no respect for his browbeaten wife, Harriet. Four years later John and Charlotte had a daughter, Ann Mary, a delight to them both. Annie, as she came to be called, was a pretty child, liked fine clothes, and became a dressmaker to the wealthy.

The second son to survive, Reuben, was more like his father; conscientious with a zest for blacksmithing, but due to a quirk of life was never able to fulfil his ambitions. On John Webster's death, Jack, being the eldest son, took it upon himself to claim the property and business as his own and now lived there with Harriet, who unhappily remained childless. Now Jack had to prove his claim to ownership.

Harriet Webster was skinning a rabbit in the kitchen of the forge cottage. She slit the carcass open, ripped the skin over the rabbit's legs, and banged a cleaver down to crack through the leg bones. The entrails she gathered up and threw out of the back door for a scavenging dog which roamed the village.

She stopped what she was doing and stood at the kitchen table with her hands on her hips watching Jack banging cupboard doors and pulling out drawers, scattering the contents on to the floor. He paused only to hitch up the loose breeches he wore and tighten the rope belt that encircled him below his fat belly; a frenzied habit that always accompanied his temper. She let him continue for a while, thinking how absurd he was, until she could stand his stupidity no longer.

'Eight years I've been married to you, Jack Webster, and the Lord knows that I have scrubbed this house thoroughly from top to bottom. I know every inch of it and I have told you there are no deeds hidden anywhere in here,' she said, projecting the cleaver in his direction to emphasize her point.

'Well, have a good look again, woman. They must be here somewhere. They can't have disappeared into thin air.'

'What do you want them for after all these years anyway?' she asked.

'Damn it, you know what for. I told you. You never listen. To prove the property and the land is mine. I'll be blowed if I'm going to pay rent to just anybody coming here and demanding money.'

'Could the deeds be somewhere in the forge?' asked Harriet, following him round the house picking up after him and tidying their possessions away back into the drawers and cupboards.

'Of course not, you foolish woman. Dad wouldn't put paper things in the forge. He'd put them somewhere in here safe and where that is, God only knows.'

'Well, they're definitely not in this house. Have you been and asked your Annie if she knows where they are? She was very close to your father, maybe he confided in her and told her what he did with them.'

'Aye, I've asked her. She knows same as me, nought. She had nothing to do with the affairs when Dad died. Her job was to help Mam,' he said, repeatedly searching through cupboards which he had already looked in at least twice before.

'Looks as if I'm now without a home then if you can't lay claim to this place,' said Harriet.

'Of course you're not without a home. I just need to find proof that Dad owned the property and I inherited it from him when he died.'

'Ye Gods, it's a right family I've married into. Can't look after their own property,' said Harriet, crossing her arms over her scrawny chest with her usual scornful look that always irritated Jack to his limits.

'Married? You don't call this a marriage do you? When was the last time you shared my bed?'

'There's more to marriage than beds, and anyway, I'd rather sleep outside in the sty with the old sow than share your bed,' said Harriet.

'You might have to do that if I don't find those deeds.'

Harriet had been born in Sussex of a good family and came to Dindley as lady's maid at the big house twenty years ago. Her father had been a butler and her mother a housekeeper in Sussex so she was quite used to the high standards that service demanded. Much different to her life now. It had been early in the marriage when Harriet felt alienated and realised she had made a big mistake by marrying a man so lacking in respect and as aggressive as Jack Webster.

His aggression had not been apparent to her before the wedding. He had hounded her, visiting the big house on any excuse and every opportunity so that he could see her, pleading with her to become his wife with promises beyond her wildest expectations. Promises that disappeared like dust on the wind after they were married. He was a man who liked to drink ale excessively and most of his money went to the innkeeper. He liked to show off and would buy drinks for all who were in the inn at the time of his visits, which were often. Too late now; she was in a situation she could not get out of, part of the Webster family. She often wondered how Lizzie would cope with such a family.

'What about Reuben? Will he know anything about the deeds?' asked Harriet.

'Oh, aye, our Reuben. Aye, it's about time I paid him and his new bride a visit. A month now they've been wed and not a word. I'll have a ride up there to Townsend Cottage. Bring m' boots here for me, woman.'

Harriet dutifully fetched his boots from the back scullery and threw them defiantly in front of him.

'How does our Reuben end up with a young filly like that Lizzie Palmer, and I have to put up with a barren hag like you?' Jack said as he struggled to pull his boots over his fat ankles.

'Because that's all you deserve,' snarled Harriet, leaning towards this man who was twice her size, her beaked nose in his face and her sunken eyes glaring at him. With that, Jack's short temper got the better of him and he lashed out with his big fist into her face, sending her staggering backwards. Harriet grabbed the cleaver from the table to defend herself. Despite her size she was not afraid of him, but he was anxious to quiz Reuben so pushed her aside and strode ungainly out of the house.

'You great big brute,' she screeched through the door after him.

'Go to the Devil, I'm going up to North Fell to see that brother of mine.'

Chapter 10

Lizzie tried to shake off the despondent feeling that was starting to overwhelm her. Over the four weeks she had been married to Reuben she had tried so hard to keep the cottage clean and tidy. It was difficult when everything was old and broken and water had to be carried in a bucket up the steep lane from the river, a longer journey now since the heat had dried up the nearby beck.

Today Reuben had set out early going north along the drovers' road to Hawes market, driving twenty sheep which he hoped to sell. This would give him enough money to buy a prize ram so that he could breed some quality into his ailing flock. His old rams had been sold to the butcher who had slaughtered them and traded the mutton in his shop in the village. Reuben would not be home until nightfall, or even the next day if the bidding at the market took a long time, so Lizzie was determined to make progress while he was away and dared to hope for some praise on his return.

As soon as Reuben was out of sight Lizzie ran across the meadows to collect enough water from the river to fill the big set pot, and she would light the fire under it like Mrs Dawson had shown her. If she took the biggest of her buckets instead of the usual-sized one it would be very heavy to carry back up the hill but she would not have to make so many journeys which would save some time.

Her flimsy shoes were no protection from the early morning dew which still lay glistening on the meadow grass, and by the time she returned with the fourth bucketful her feet were wet and sore. She was tired and her wrenched shoulders ached, but her determination to please Reuben and the thought of toasting her toes once she had the fire roaring to heat the water kept her going.

In the scullery, she struggled to tilt and pour the contents of the last bucketful into the set pot and was startled by pounding on the front door so loud that she dropped the bucket. The precious water spilled and spread out across the floor like an opening fan. Heeding Reuben's instructions that no one was to come into the cottage she opened the door cautiously, just far enough to be able to see the outline of a big man who she recognized as Reuben's brother; Jack Webster the blacksmith.

'Mr Webster, you banged so hard I thought the door would surely break.'

'Open the door, Lizzie, and let me in.'

'No, I mustn't let anyone in. What do you want here?'

'Come on, Lizzie, let me in. I must speak to our Reuben.'

'No, you can't.'

'Tell him I must see him now, straight away. It's important.'

'He's not here just now. Go away.'

Lizzie tried to close the door, but before she could engage the latch Jack lifted his knee and, holding each side of the door frame for balance, propelled his big boot forward, knocking the door out of Lizzie's hands and off its hinges. It landed flat on the kitchen floor, sending a cloud of ash from the open hearth into the room to meet the water which had spilled from the set pot.

'Now look what you've done! What a mess. Are you drunk?'

'No, I'm not drunk and I must see our Reuben at once. Where is he? It's a matter of great importance he might be able to help me with.'

'He's out, about his business. I'll tell him that you called and if you explain to me what's so important I'll let him know when he returns.'

'It's not for your pretty little ears,' said Jack, moving close to her and touching her hair. 'Will it be long before he comes in?'

'You'll have to come back tomorrow. He's gone to Hawes market and me now without a door to protect myself.'

'So, it's protection you want. I best stop a while then. I can look after you.'

'I fancy not,' said Lizzie, who was starting to feel very confused and not quite sure that he should be standing so close to her. Moving away from him she reached for a broom and started to sweep some of the ash back into the hearth.

'I'm very busy, Mr Webster, and I'm sure you have plenty to do. I should like you to leave now. Good day, Mr Webster,' Lizzie said, directing him towards the door.

He put his hand on her shoulder and held her firmly, slowly running his fingers down her arm.

'Get away from me, Jack Webster!'

'Come on, Lizzie. I want a share of what our Reuben's getting.' He grabbed her hair and pulled her head back, pushing his hairy face forward towards her, a wild look in his eyes like a savage animal. She flinched as she caught the nauseating stench of his foul breath. She tried to move away but he held her tight in his grip.

'I'm warning you,' she said, still trying to push him aside, but her arms ached from carrying the buckets of water and the little strength she still had was no match against a man of Jack's size. She was horrified by his sudden, wild behaviour, amazed how quickly he had become so hostile.

He threw her down on to the alcove bed. His large frame towered above her and the width of his brawny body in the narrow alcove opening left no escape route past him. He quickly unknotted the rope belt from his waist and let his breeches fall. His big hands fumbled and tore at her clothes.

Lizzie screamed and shouted and fought for her life, but his fat, sweaty body covered her completely and she could not move or breathe. With each rhythmic thrust into her he growled like an angry dog. She thought the painful ordeal would never end and she would surely suffocate.

'Oh, you glorious creature,' he breathlessly whispered in her ear. When eventually he rolled off the little bed, he threw her aside like a rag doll. He waddled across the kitchen over the fallen door while hitching up his breeches. He kept up a good pace down the lane, adjusting his shirt and knotting the rope belt as he ran.

Lizzie lay motionless on the bed for a long time, her knees drawn up to her chest, whimpering, traumatised. She could not understand how this man she had known and trusted for years could attack her so callously. She had often enjoyed watching him in the forge while he worked. Seen how gently he stroked the horses while the hoof remained firm in his leathered lap. He had let her pump the big bellows. In winter she had warmed herself over the cinders and roasted chestnuts in the dying embers.

Now he had made her feel worthless and so desperately alone in this ungodly, isolated place she had got herself into. Only once before in her life had Lizzie ever felt so alone, so distraught, and visions of her mother came flooding back. The flames, her mother's hair on fire, powdery shreds of her clothes floating from her body, her arms reaching out to her children as she tried to climb the stairs to get to them. The screams and the long wait, naked, when nobody emerged from the raging fire. She had thought she could never feel so desolate as she had that night, but here again was the same unbearable feeling.

Chapter 11

'All right, Lizzie, I'm sorry, I shouldn't have lost my temper,' said Reuben. 'But you've been sulking now for two weeks. Ever since the day I went to Hawes market. I did warn you I'd be late getting back.'

'I'm not sulking,' said Lizzie.

'Yes you are. You haven't spoken to me for days or done any work. You've just sat on that bed with your nose in those damn books of yours. There's no food prepared. What am I supposed to eat?'

It was true she had tried to get comfort from her books but she had just gazed at page after page and not consciously absorbed a word. She wanted to tell Reuben what had happened and why she felt so wretched. She had rehearsed the conversation over and over in her head but could not bring herself to tell him that it had been his own brother, Jack, who had been so brutal and done this to her. That it was Jack who had seen her as a woman and taken her so violently. That it was Jack who had kicked the door down and not her excuse that the wind had blown it in. If Reuben had taken the trouble to think about it there had been no wind that day, it had been calm and sultry, but his mind had been racing ahead on other things. He wanted to forget the past. The farm had potential and the prospects excited him, but he knew it was going to take lot of hard work. He just wanted Lizzie to be as enthusiastic as he was and now he was beginning to wish he had taken more time looking for a wife and chosen a more mature woman.

'Look lass, I can't run this farm on my own,' he said quietly, trying to explain and hoping Lizzie would understand the difficult situation they were in. 'You must do your share of the work. There's more than enough work here for the two of us. Now I know why Widow Learoyd insisted that I take a wife.'

'But I'm not a wife. Am I?'

'No, you're not. You've become an extra burden for me to carry.'

'I've become no more than a servant in this ramshackle house,' she said.

'For goodness' sake, get yourself off that bed and do some work before I throw every one of those books into the fire.' He grabbed her arm and dragged her off the bed to her feet, shaking her and hoping she would see sense. Lizzie struggled to free herself but she was tight in his grip like an animal in a trap.

'Ow, let go of me, you're hurting my arm.' She was no match to him in an argument and, much to her annoyance, was near tears. The injustice she felt made her want to run from this frightful place. Just to run and keep running as far away as she could. Now, too late, she realised she should have given some serious thought about entering into this marriage instead of rushing into it thinking all her dreams would come true. She knew now that she should have asked to see the house first and ask what was expected of her.

He marched her into the scullery where the loom set in one corner dominated the room. The stone floor was almost covered with rolls of fleece which Reuben had neatly stacked.

'This pile of wool is for you to deal with. I spent days shearing until my back ached so much I could hardly stand, but you don't care. We have no money, Lizzie. Widow Learoyd left me the farm but she didn't leave me any money, not a penny. This is how we have to make our money, from the sheep. You spinning and me weaving as fast as we can.' He flung her down on to the pile of fleece. 'Now make a start.'

Lizzie sat among the rolls of fleece, rubbing her arm and glaring up at him indignantly. She had no idea how to make a start. To her, sheep were food. She knew how to cook a piece of mutton and make a delicious meal from most parts of the carcass, but the fleece meant nothing to her.

'They're all dirty and they smell,' she said, convinced this must be some sort of penance the Lord had placed upon her for her stupid scheming to get a husband. It had only been wishful thinking, she had not meant to be evil and very much regretted her actions now that she had reaped the consequences.

'Well, take them all to the river and wash them. Then you need to card the fibres and prepare wool for me to weave. That's not asking too much, is it?'

'I don't know how to do all that,' she said.

Not wanting to admit he did not know either, Reuben resorted to aggression before Lizzie could ask him to show her how. 'Doesn't it tell you how in those books of yours?'

'No. They're not that sort of book, they're more intellectual,' she said.

'Oh my word, intellectual,' Reuben scoffed. 'So much for your fancy learning. What good are your books to you now? You'll have to pay a visit to our Annie and ask if she'll give you some lessons.'

The thought of having her haughty sister-in-law meddling in her life again added to her misery, but she could not think of anyone else who could help her.

Reuben and Lizzie continued to argue and their bickering was so intensive that they had not noticed the stranger approaching the cottage.

'Are you there?' A gruff shout halted their noisy hostilities. Both looked up, taken unawares and not used to uninvited visitors. A train of four packhorses flanked the cobbles outside the front door; the lead rein held loosely over the shoulder of a small, bent figure of a man whose crooked back was covered in a square of oilskin.

'Are you there?' he repeated in an accent not akin to either Reuben or Lizzie.

'And who are you? What do you want?' snapped Reuben.

'I'm travelling and buying as I go along, but for the last hour I've been watching the dark storm cloud approaching over the hill. It'll be here any moment and I came looking for shelter until it passes. I didn't realise anyone would be living up here. It looked so derelict.'

Reuben looked up at the storm belt above the bleak moor top. The mass of black swirling cloud looked spectacular against the clear azure sky and the brilliance of the sun still shining on the valley. There had been weeks of hot dry weather, beautiful cloudless days, but the hay was safely in now so some gentle rain would be more than welcome. He could hear rumbles of thunder in the distance and all the birds had gone to ground. A tumultuous wind, already blowing ahead of the rain, showed signs of a storm too violent to be effective on the parched ground. A sudden deafening crack and a blinding flash of lightning had the stranger fighting to control his frightened horses.

'I suppose you might be able to squeeze in the old byre here,' said Reuben, pulling away overgrown ivy and weeds from the byre door and dragging it open. 'I've never used it myself but it should suffice for an hour. There's no feed or water though for them there 'osses of yours. My stock are out on the moor fending for themselves.'

'It'll do. Then I'll be on my way,' said the stranger.

'What do you buy?' asked Reuben.

'Most things, depending on the time of year. Today I'm buying fleece for the worsted weavers.'

'I deal in fleece. I might be able to find a few to sell to you,' Reuben said, trying to sound expert in the trade and steering the conversation to gain the knowledge he lacked. 'In your travels have you come across anything new for washing fleece?'

'No. The old ways are tried and tested, they'll not change.'

'Aye, you're right. We have our own ways here. Which are the old ways from where you come from?'

'The contents of your chamber pot, good and strong. Can't beat it. Still the best.'

'Disgusting,' said Lizzie, screwing up her face as if she had just bitten into a sour apple.

'Be quiet, Lizzie. Go back in the house and attend to your work.'

The stranger saw that Lizzie was repulsed by the idea and realised Reuben's conversation was not characteristic of an experienced shepherd.

Once the horses were settled, Reuben showed the stranger into the scullery to see if a deal could be struck. Picking up the rolls of fleece one by one and rubbing them through his fingers he could not believe such a fine, dense quality could be got from sheep running wild on moorland. He perceived there was a bargain to be made here.

'Ooh, poor quality,' said the stranger, pulling at the crimp then throwing them back down, frowning and shaking his head. 'Fibres too short. I'm looking for long staple wool, that's what the worsted weavers want. I suppose I could take a few off your hands.'

Lizzie, who was listening from the kitchen, hoped he would take the lot.

'Can't give you much,' he said but Reuben, desperately in need of money, took the first offer presented to him. He foolishly trusted this man who assured him so convincingly that he would not get a better price from buyers at any market. A 'few' became most of Reuben's stockpile, leaving just three dozen fleeces for Lizzie to practise spinning and him to perfect his weaving.

The storm passed and, with his packhorses weighed down, the buyer bid Reuben farewell and left thinking he had done a good day's trading all in one go. The strong wind and torrential rain had battered the cottage, leaving clues as to where the roof leaked and badly needed repairing, but at least the nearby beck was running again.

Chapter 12

'We need to skirt it first. That's cutting all the soiled bits away around the tail end and underneath. The best wool is across the shoulder and then down the sides,' said Annie, who was reluctantly spending the day at Townsend Cottage to give Lizzie her first lesson. Her dependable horse and trap had not been able to drive up the steep, narrow lane to the cottage so she'd had to return home and walk the two miles from her house. On arrival she vowed she would not be visiting again.

They were both down on their knees looking closely at the large fleece which, stretched out, covered most of the kitchen floor. Annie pointed out the best and worst areas and explained the texture, fineness, fibres and crimp. Lizzie felt very daunted, both by Annie and by this mass laid out prostrate before her, but she remained quiet and willing to learn. Reuben, with money in his pocket, could not wait to spend it. He thought it was better to get out of the way and leave them to their tuition so made the excuse that he would spend the day visiting neighbouring farms to buy himself a pig.

With sufficient wool collected, the job of scouring and washing was next. To Lizzie's relief the urine was diluted with three parts water which made the process a little less unsavoury, and when rinsed in the beck became bearable to handle although still slightly greasy with a little lanolin remaining in it.

'This is really good quality fleece,' said Annie. 'Leaving the sheep to winter up on the moor has produced some thick coats.'

'Oh, Reuben thought they were poor and not worth much,' said Lizzie.

'He obviously doesn't know how to judge a good fleece. If he had a mind to sell them he could get a good price for these. Any buyer would snap them up.'

Lizzie kept quiet, not mentioning that he had already sold some. She thought she would keep this information to herself and delight in picking her moment to tell Reuben that he should not have let his temper get the better of him and should have waited for other prices to compare instead of selling in haste.

'Steady, not so rough. Comb it through the cards quickly but gently. Watch me, do it like this,' said Annie, giving Lizzie the next stage of her lesson. Lizzie looked at Annie's hands. They were so small and pretty, soft and glove-white, and she stroked the cards together quickly to prepare the wool ready for spinning. When Lizzie tried to do it she felt as if her own rough hands had grown to twice their size and thought Annie was sure to tell her about the dirt beneath her fingernails. Progressing to the drop spindle was just as laborious. It looked so easy when Annie was showing her but Lizzie found it difficult to tease out the fleece and twist the spindle at the same time.

'I could do with an extra pair of hands,' said Lizzie.

'Just watch me again and remember which way to turn the spindle. Your left hand does this and the right does this.' Annie demonstrated once more, but by this time it was late afternoon and she departed, leaving Lizzie to practise on her own.

Lizzie persevered and soon improved, getting quicker until the day came when she had enough wool washed and carded ready for her next lesson on the spinning wheel which was to be at Annie's house. With a large parcel of prepared wool under her arm, she set off from the cottage down the steep lane towards the village. When she got to the little packhorse bridge the parcel was becoming too heavy and she had no hesitation in dropping it to the ground and resting for a while.

A kingfisher sat on a branch at the water's edge but darted away as soon as Lizzie approached. The hump of the bridge was an ideal place to lean over and watch the fish swimming in the clear water below. She was in no hurry to get to Annie's house and delayed the ordeal as long as possible by watching a dipper perched on a stone bobbing his tail up and down and dipping his body, then disappearing beneath the water and reappearing again. From here she could see the forge on the other side of the river which she would have to walk past to get to Annie's house. She made sure that Jack was nowhere in sight before she continued along the drovers' road into Dindley village.

She had never been through the little wooden gate to Annie's house before but had often read the sign that was nailed to it, 'Miss Webster, Dressmaker of Distinction'. The cinders on the path running the length of the long garden crunched under her feet as she walked with trepidation towards the door. The garden was planted with herbs, and the pleasant sweet smell they released had a calming effect and helped a little to dispel some of the nervousness she felt. Lizzie thought she would make a garden one day and sit there taking in the fragrance and watching the sunset.

Annie showed Lizzie into the front parlour which was arranged as a sewing room. A screen across one corner served as a partitioned fitting area. A tailor's dummy stood in the middle of the floor and dominated the room, ostentatiously wearing a beautiful dark-green, low-cut gown that was destined to grace some ballroom of grandeur. There were bolts of fabrics of various colours and textures all neatly shelved around the room.

Annie watched in horror as Lizzie started rummaging in awe among the bobbins and ribbons, rubbing the materials between her grubby fingers and making coo-cooing noises like a nesting pigeon.

'Leave all those things alone. Put that down. Don't touch anything,' Annie said, frantically retrieving things and putting them back in their rightful places.

'Pardon me,' Lizzie said, taking a step backwards and biting her bottom lip.

'Sit there,' said Annie, pointing to a stool in a corner of the room next to the spinning wheel. 'I must first put the finishing touches to this pair of gloves I've made. Someone will be calling for them very shortly.'

Lizzie sat very still on the appointed seat. The spinning wheel stood at her side like a demon waiting to take possession of her soul, and as Annie sewed Lizzie became increasingly uncomfortable. When the gloves were finished, Annie packed them in a box, wrapped it in brown paper, and tied it up with string ready to be collected. She joined Lizzie at the spinning wheel in the corner and proceeded to demonstrate another of her never-ending skills.

'Oh heck, I'll never do it as good as you,' said Lizzie.

'Yes you will. It's not complicated. Any child can do it.'

There was that word again. Child. Lizzie clenched her teeth but remained silent. She was still eager to learn but the motion of the wheel spinning made her feel dizzy and she moved uneasily on the stool. The feeling did not pass and she just had to get out of there into the fresh air.

'I'll have to go home,' she blurted out.

'Well, don't suppose I'm anxious to keep you. I have plenty to occupy myself and I sense you aren't really interested in becoming skilful at anything that will be profitable for you and Reuben.'

'Oh, I am, I am, but I don't feel like myself this morning,' said Lizzie.

'Very well. You do look a little pale.'

'I really feel very faint. I think it best if I make my way home.'

'I expect you're overcome by the heat and the long walk. You mustn't think of leaving the cottage until you are fully recovered.' Annie splashed a few drops of lavender water on to a white handkerchief and handed it to Lizzie.

'Try this. It always revives me when the heat becomes too much.'

'Thank you. You're very kind but it is not the heat making me feel so wretched.'

'I suspect then that happily there's a baby,' said Annie.

'Of course it's a baby, and sadly it isn't of Reuben's making.'

Lizzie let the words slip, realising all too late that she should not have said that. The last person she wanted to know of her predicament was Annie, but she did feel some sense of relief now someone shared her burden.

'Well, I never. I'm ashamed to look at you,' said Annie.

Lizzie jumped to her feet, protesting loudly. 'No, no you don't understand!'

'Oh yes I do. I understand all right. I had my suspicions that you were up to mischief when you married our Reuben. You've just made a convenience of him.'

'I don't deserve that. There are circumstances you know nothing about.'

'Pray go on. Enlighten me to these circumstances that you've no doubt concocted in your mind.'

Lizzie was outraged that she was being blamed and without stopping to think defended herself. 'It was Jack Webster, your Jack. It was Jack. He used me brutally just to spite Reuben. He came to the cottage when I was all alone there. I tried with what little strength I had to fight him off but he was much too strong for me.'

Silence followed this alarming outburst. Annie was not quite sure whether to believe her and sat bewildered, the blatant statement going over and over in her mind. Lizzie turned and stood looking out of the window, fighting the anger within her.

When she had calmed herself, but still unable to turn and face Annie, she told her the full story. How Jack had broken the door and forced his way into the cottage against her wishes and how frightened she had been. How he had imposed himself on her and how he had ripped her clothes. How she had fought him with all her strength but had been overcome. How for days afterwards the intensity of his wickedness had affected her and caused her and Reuben to quarrel.

'You can't imagine how I feel,' said Lizzie. 'How can I tell Reuben what he did? I just want to die.'

Annie felt so ashamed that it was her own brother who had

wantonly inflicted this misery upon this young girl. Jack Webster, the eldest of the three siblings, whose responsibility it should have been to take charge and hold the family together by example, was now to be more of an outcast than he already was. Annie had had little patience with Lizzie in the past. She had considered her to be weak and not worthy of their family. Now those sad eyes were looking at her like a wounded animal unable to help itself, and Annie just wanted to protect her as best she could.

'Come, sit here with me,' said Annie, holding out her hand. The hand was a welcome sight, the first sign of friendship Lizzie had received, and she took it willingly. She had never needed a friend so much as she did right now.

'Does anyone else know about this?' asked Annie.

Lizzie shook her head.

'We must work out what we're going to do. Are you quite sure what you have told me is the truth?'

'Oh yes. It's true. Every word.'

'Then God help us if Reuben finds out,' said Annie. 'There'd be trouble beyond belief. Reuben would kill him. Then where would we be? One dead and the other hanged or transported away to goodness knows where. Reuben must never, *never* find out that the child is not his. You must never tell him. This will be our secret.'

Chapter 13

Dindley Hall stood to the west at the head of the dale some distance from the centre of the village. Constructed in the early eighteenth century during an intense period of national building, the plans and records of the hall were vague and the architect unknown. It was thought that the squire was descended from the French Gourney family and the hall had been erected in the French style by his prosperous ancestors. This extreme style had been altered, simplified and added to over the years by various ancestors; the stable block being the latest addition.

When visited in his room, the groom, who had fallen from his horse the previous day, was found lying rigid with eyes closed and uttering intermittent groans which increased in severity when any visitors approached the head of his bed. Having suddenly remembered, late in the afternoon, that her new gloves should have been collected from her dressmaker, My Lady had decided to collect the parcel herself and exercise her horse at the same time. A request for the groom to saddle My Lady's horse resulted in a weak dismissive wave of his hand so Tom, the gamekeeper, was to take over his duties and ride along with her as chaperone.

Word was sent to the courtyard that she had changed into her riding habit and was now sweeping down the wide staircase of the house, running her whip along the twisted baluster railing, the noisy rat-a-tat heralding her warning, to whomever, to get out of her way. It was a simple walk across the courtyard to the stable block where she would expect her horse to be saddled and ready however short a warning they'd had to prepare it.

In the absence of the groom, the gamekeeper was attempting to saddle two horses. Shouting, fuss and bustle, pumping of water, and hurried grooming from helping hands accompanied his attempts. He was looking forward to the journey, it would be an excuse to see Annie; his beloved Annie.

They trotted through the large gateway, an ideal place to start a ride out, then kept up a steady canter following the meandering river until My Lady decided to race ahead, her scarf flying behind her like a flag blowing in the wind. Tom kept his distance behind until they reached Annie's cottage; he knew better than to try and race her, although he knew she would have found it exciting.

'No need for you to dismount, My Lady. I'll go in and quickly collect the parcel for you,' said Tom, handing the reins of his horse quickly across to her to hold before she could refuse the offer. She watched him walk with a confident swagger up the path of Annie's house, whistling nonchalantly as he approached the door. He was invited in and it was quite some time before he reappeared.

'You've been a long time, Thomas. The horses were getting restless.'

'Sorry to leave you unattended, My Lady. The gloves were not quite ready. Annie still had some stitching to finish and make up the parcel.'

Quite rightly she did not believe a word but secretly admired him for his audacity. He was an attractive man with eyes which would melt any woman's heart. She would not have tolerated such behaviour from any other of her staff.

'Don't forget, Thomas, you are a married man.'

'Carpe diem, my lady, carpe diem,' he smirked, showing no sign of guilt or shame.

Chapter 14

There were just six rungs to the loft ladder. Six simple wooden steps which stood in front of Lizzie like a towering precipice blocking the way to Reuben's bed. A frightening climb she knew she must conquer if any solution was to be found to the predicament she was in. She had not revealed everything to Annie. She had not told her that Reuben would know this baby inside her was not his because she did not lie with him in his bed at night, nor had she ever done so. The violation and pain of the rape were still so vivid in her mind, every deplorable moment carved into her memory, and the immense revulsion she felt would be hard to overcome. Even if she could do that she still had to find a way to discard the childlike image Reuben had of her in order to arouse his interest. It was going to take great effort and deceit and must be done without delay.

Reuben rose early from his bed and let the pig into the orchard to feed on the windfall apples before setting off on the long walk across the moors to attend to his sheep. The fellside was high above the dawn mist which still covered the lowland and river like a gossamer web. He loved this time of day when the yellow morning light blended with the purple haze of the heather. He rested for a while, listening to the curlews' cry dueting the bleat of his lambs. A previous sighting of a fox had made him very anxious. A hungry vixen was very brazen and would stand her ground; without a dog or gun he would not be much of a deterrent.

Alone in the cottage Lizzie seized the opportunity to practise climbing the dreaded ladder. Somehow she had to get to the top and into Reuben's bed. All day she tried. First she managed two rungs.

Then, after plucking up all her courage, closing her eyes, and clenching her teeth, she managed to drag herself up on to the third. Again regaining her determination she tried for the fourth but she just could not take that next step. No matter how much she told herself she must do it and it was the only solution to her problem, she still could not move above that third rung.

She was dangling there when Reuben, returning home early, came bursting through the door. She dropped to the floor suddenly with a thud, flustered and embarrassed, but he was in a bad temper and did not notice the flush to her face. She straightened her dress and tossed her head back, trying to look as if she was about her work as usual.

'Oh, Reuben, you're home so soon,' she said, acting out the normality.

'Lizzie, do you not listen to anything I say?' he shouted. 'The pig is still in the orchard. I asked you to walk it down to Old Will Scaife's farm for him to put it with his boar.' There was anger in his face, the set of his jaw and pursed lips that Lizzie had become familiar with was upsetting and she knew she would have to ply very hard for his affections after this mistake.

'I did,' she lied. 'Old Will wasn't there.'

'Well, couldn't you have put it with the boar yourself and left it there, save you trailing all the way back again with it? You never think do you, Lizzie?'

'I've heard that boar of his is a savage beast. I'm not going anywhere near it. You'll have to take it.'

'Don't be ridiculous. I have too much to do. You'll have to take it right now. He'll have been waiting all day for you. I'm going down to the river. I've seen a big trout up at the top end. I'm going to try and catch it. We'll have to have something to eat tonight. It doesn't look as if you've prepared anything. I don't know what you do with your day, nothing seems to get done.'

Lizzie set off down the lane and across the bridge on the long walk to Will Scaife's farm with a suitable stick in her hand. She took her frustration out on the squealing pig, giving it a hard whack every time it strayed from the path. Arriving at the farm was as much a relief to the long-suffering pig as it was to Lizzie.

The farmyard was unusually quiet; just a few chickens scratching about in the dust, and a couple of cows lowing mournfully at the dairy door waiting to be milked.

'Will,' Lizzie shouted. 'Will Scaife, 'r ya there?'

The farmhouse door was open and, looking inside, she shouted again. The house was all neat and tidy with the kitchen table prepared ready for a meal and a cauldron boiling over the fire cooking something which smelt very appetising, but there was no reply to her shouts.

'Will,' Lizzie shouted up the stairs. 'Will, I've brought Reuben's pig.' Still no answer.

She wandered about from shed to shed, calling and dreading the thought that she would have to open the sty where the boar was and deposit her pig herself. She waited with apprehension, hoping someone would appear. Returning home with the pig would upset Reuben even more and she realised there was no alternative but to deal with this herself if she were to please him. So she gave the pig another whack and pointed it in the direction of the sty across the yard. Coming from behind the grey stone wall of the pigsty, Lizzie could hear repugnant guttural noises and she hoped the sounds meant the boar was occupied eating and the distraction meant she would be safe from its alleged savagery.

The wooden door of the sty was already partially open, though not quite wide enough to push her pig through; she would have to open it wider. Through the gap she could see the huge shape of the boar, head down with its snout sunk into the mud and greedily eating. Slowly she nudged the door open a little wider, trying not to disturb the feasting brute within. At first Lizzie was not quite sure what she saw inside the sty. On closer inspection she was horrified to see the breeches of a man lying in the mud. Venturing further into the sty, she could see the boar was gnawing on the back of the man's head; the face had already been completely eaten away.

The distracted boar looked up, its cheeks stained red and blood dripping from its mouth. The man's body seemed to move. An arm slowly lifted and a ghostly hand reached out spread fingers as if asking for help. Lizzie just stared at the pleading hand, unable to move, transfixed as if a spike had been driven through her body, its sharp point staking her to the ground. The boar, attracted by the sexual offering, rushed out of the sty towards the submissive pig. Lizzie, jolted back to reality by the animal rushing towards her, fled, leaving her pig to its own destiny.

The meadow sloped steeply down to the river and Reuben lay in the heat-browned grass beneath the long arched branches of a willow tree, one hand dangling loosely in the cool water. It was the stretch where he had seen the good-sized trout, but had never been able to catch it.

The sun shone on the surface of the water and he could see the silver silhouette of the elusive fish gliding among the rounded pebbles on the river bed. It was a fine trout which would make a substantial meal. He could almost smell the aroma of it cooking and taste the delicate flesh. He lay very still, willing the creature to swim to him and determined it would not get away this time. It was almost in his hand when he heard Lizzie shouting.

He cursed at the sight of her running full speed down the field toward him, stumbling, her legs buckling under her because they would not carry her quickly enough down the slope. Thinking the excitable girl was again playing her silly games, he knew he only had seconds before the fish would be startled and dart away. He took a chance and quickly flicked the trout out of the water, successfully landing it on the grass bank at his side.

'Yes,' he gleefully shouted, his arms up in the air, pleased with his conquest and forgetting his annoyance. Mistaking Lizzie's panic-stricken cries, he joined in what he thought was her game. He grabbed hold of her and laughed and danced, lifting her off her feet and swinging her round and round.

'Put me down, I have something to tell you,' she screeched, banging her fists on his shoulders.

'Yippeeee,' he boisterously shouted, revelling in the success of his catch. He continued to spin her round with such vigour that they both lost their balance and fell to the ground, arms around each other, Reuben laughing, and Lizzie struggling to make him listen.

She was shaking uncontrollably, still in shock, and clung tightly to him out of sheer fright. He was spontaneously aroused by the womanly shape and the closeness of her body. Pleasantly surprised, he misunderstood her traumatic state as affection. Placing the flat of his hand against the small of her back he pulled her in towards him. Lizzie was still struggling, trying to tell him what she had seen, but he was not listening. He put a finger across her lips to stop her talking. He kissed her gently, brushing her black hair away from her damp tear-stained face. Again, gasping to regain her breath, she tried to tell him that Old Will Scaife lay in the sty half eaten by his pig, but her open mouth made him more excited and on impulse he kissed her with even more passion. He lifted her skirt and touched the soft inside of her thighs. He had never before noticed the blueness of her eyes; they were like a cloudless summer sky, but wide open, full of terror, and awash with tears. He had a sense of unease, thinking he'd had this effect on her, but an overwhelming desire had come over him and, although sympathetic to her feelings, in his heightened state, there was no stopping.

'It's all right, Lizzie, don't be frightened. I won't hurt you. Just stay still.'

The intrusive touch of his hand was like the rape happening all over again, but she was exhausted mentally and physically and could not find the strength to struggle any more. She tightened every muscle in her body and lay back, closed her eyes, and waited for the brutality and the pain to start, but she found the encounter tolerable with Reuben. He showed respect and repeatedly asked if he was hurting her.

As the afternoon drifted away they lay quietly side by side in the meadow among the buttercups and fragrant meadowsweet, neither of them knowing quite what to say to each other. It was only later that Lizzie realised what he had unwittingly done. Relieved, she just hoped that Annie could be trusted never to reveal her secret deceit.

It was evening before Lizzie recovered from the traumas of the day and composed herself sufficiently to tell Reuben about the dreadful scene she had witnessed. She had never seen him so angry, almost striking her for not telling him straight away. He ran all the way to the Scaifes' farm but was too late. It was Old Will's half-eaten dead body that he recovered from the sty.

Lizzie looked at the lifeless trout lying on the kitchen table; its mouth stiffly open as if screaming and its glassy pensive eyes staring at her and seeming to watch her every move. *Could this be my saviour?*

While Reuben was away she could prepare and cook it and again try to please him by having it ready for him on his return home. She covered its eyes and used a knife to stab it open, apologising unceremoniously to the slippery creature. She took the gutted fish to the beck and washed it in the cool fresh water, then gathered watercress, dandelion and wild thyme which grew in the damp ground. Back in the kitchen she chopped and mixed the herbs with veal forcemeat and stuffed the empty cavity for extra flavour. Cooked to perfection, the fish was plated on the table when Reuben returned. It was very late and the nausea he felt, caused by what he had found at the farm, gave him no appetite for food. He did not speak. His furrowed brow emphasised the glare of disgust as he climbed the ladder to his bed, leaving Lizzie once more defeated.

Chapter 15

The hammock, securely suspended from the thick branches of the old oak tree at the bottom of the garden, swung slowly from side to side in the gentle afternoon breeze. A wool blanket lined the canvas and was loosely wrapped round the occupant who slept a laudanum-induced sleep. Inside the house Mr Fothergill broke off from working at his desk and strode across the floor to answer a knock at the door, but Lizzie was already letting herself in. It was a strange feeling for her, being in the house again; vaguely familiar, just like coming home.

'Where's your butler?' she joked. 'I expected at least to be shown into the parlour.'

'Lizzie, I'm so pleased to see you but stop being facetious. He doesn't attend to the same kind of duties that you used to do.'

'Yes, but where is he? You seem to hide him away. I would like to meet him.'

'He said he'd seen a weed in the garden that he couldn't identify and was going to have another look at it, but I know different. In fact he's not at all well and is resting in the hammock. I'm quite worried at his condition and pray daily for his recovery.'

'Maybe I could have a drink to refresh myself after my long walk here. I came along the river path, a much longer way round but a much prettier walk, don't you agree?' She did not admit that she had taken that route to avoid passing the forge where she might have come face to face with Jack Webster. She still feared the man and what he might do if she placed herself in a vulnerable position.

'Yes, a much rewarding walk and of course you must have a drink. I've been so engrossed in my work that I hadn't noticed the hour. It's almost time for tea anyway.'

'Then I shall make a drink for both of us, if I can remember where everything is kept. Then we can sit down and talk and I can tell you my news. Shall I take a tray to the hammock?' asked Lizzie, still wishing to meet this mysterious man.

'No, he's best left to sleep. The doctor has been and aided him with a mixture.'

Mr Fothergill had long thought of Lizzie as the daughter he would never have so he always had time to sit and listen to her gossip and, always concerned for her welfare, hoped she had brought good news. She had waited a suitable length of time before visiting but could no longer put off announcing her condition. Returning from the kitchen with the tea tray, she poured two cups while telling him there was to be a springtime baby.

'I'm delighted, my dear. Now your home will be complete, your own little family you've always longed for. But you don't look very happy. Is something troubling you?'

She could not tell him of the dreadful secret she was hiding and that she was tormented day and night by an overwhelming feeling of hatred for the unwanted creature inside her. 'I don't know how we'll manage,' she said, 'but Reuben is condescending and says as long as we both work hard and God is willing, we'll get along somehow.'

'I'm sure you will. Now what else has been happening?' he asked, dismissing Lizzie's expected news as domestic trivia.

'Well,' said Lizzie, relieved to talk of other matters and so reducing the chance of giving away her secret, and settled down into a big armchair which engulfed her, 'Jack Webster, it appears, is in somewhat of a quandary.'

Mr Fothergill carefully blotted the wet ink on the school accounts he had been working on, closed the big leather-bound ledger, and placed it in the desk drawer, closed the ink well, and cleaned the quill pen. He sat down heavily in the armchair opposite Lizzie, and picked up his cup of tea, ready to listen.

'Go on,' he said. 'What do you mean, a quandary? I'm eager to know.'

'Well, the bailiffs have been to the forge.' She chattered rapidly now she had his full attention and wriggled into the big soft cushions on the armchair, tucking her legs up under her.

'Sit in that chair properly, Lizzie, you're not a child any more, you're a young lady now and must conduct yourself as such.'

Obediently Lizzie's feet returned to the floor and she sat straight-backed on the edge of the chair. She liked being called a young lady instead of a child at last, but sensed the interruption to her story had caused it to lose momentum.

'That's better. Now take a deep breath and speak slowly and precisely. You were saying something about the bailiffs at the forge.'

'Yes, they returned yesterday to the forge to remind Jack they'd be returning on Michaelmas Day and he was to have rent ready for them to collect. One hundred pounds I believe.'

'And is Jack going to pay them one hundred pounds?'

Mrs Dawson said there was a lot of shouting and swearing between the men. Jack Webster told them he hadn't got one hundred pounds and wasn't going to pay them anyway, so they gave him notice to leave immediately and find somewhere else to live.

'This information has come from Mrs Dawson, you said. Is it reliable then or is it is likely to be just her usual fabricated gossip?'

'Oh no, it's true. Jack insists the property is his, inherited from his father, but he can't find the deeds to prove it. He's searched everywhere and Reuben and Annie can't help him.'

'He'll never find them,' said Mr Fothergill. 'The forge, cottage and everything near was a jointure in favour of Widow Learoyd. That means it all became hers, some years ago, after the death of her husband. John Webster, Reuben and Jack's father, only rented the property from her. He never owned the forge or any of it.'

'Well, I wonder why Jack didn't know anything of this. He's frantic trying to find evidence that the place is his, and it never was, you say.'

'That's right,' Mr Fothergill confirmed.

'So Widow Learoyd has the deeds, or rather her family have them now since her death.'

'Yes, the whole of the property was only rented. It was a private arrangement between Widow Learoyd and John Webster. It was kept very quiet, there weren't many people who knew about it, but I was one of the witnesses to the deal. I was sworn to secrecy.'

'But why? Why was it kept quiet?' Lizzie asked.

'No money changed hands. It wasn't a financial deal. An agreement was drawn up that the rent was to be one red rose on mid-summer's day. So you must form your own conclusion from that.'

'Oh, that was very generous of her,' Lizzie said giggling. 'I conclude there must have been something more to it than that.'

'Yes, John Webster and Mrs Learoyd, before her marriage, were very much in love. They'd been childhood sweethearts, but she wasn't allowed to marry him. He wasn't considered suitable by her father. A more suitable marriage was arranged for her to marry a cousin, one who would keep all the wealth within the family. By the time her husband died and left her the property in her own right, Jack was married to someone else.'

'How romantic, one red rose every mid-summer's day. But how sad too,' said Lizzie.

'I must talk to Jack at once, explain the situation, and advise him what to do,' said Mr Fothergill. 'Under the circumstances he must be given a Letter of Licence allowing him a longer, more reasonable, period of time for the payment to be made.'

'No need for you to bother, Mr Fothergill, I'll tell him. I'll call at the forge on my way home and explain the whole situation to him and tell him to visit you for your advice.'

The sun was setting and the air had turned cold as Lizzie left Mr Fothergill's house. She wished she had brought her shawl but still walked home along the river path, the longer way, to again avoid the forge. Feeling exalted, with no intention of telling Jack what she had learned, she had a little skip in her step. She wanted to watch him squirm for as long as possible.

Chapter 16

Dindley was changing colour. The leaves had turned to rustic shades of orange, brown and red, and were now starting to fall. Grass had lost its scorched, dry appearance and had sprouted new green shoots. The heather had finished flowering and the purple haze on the moor had faded. Flocks of birds, preparing for their flight to warmer climes, were soaring like handfuls of dust thrown into a grey and misty sky.

The mood at Townsend Cottage had not changed. This should have been a happy season, settling down and improving their lifestyle, and preparing for the long winter months ahead, but Reuben continued to find fault with most of the things that Lizzie did. Unforgiving, he long held her to blame for the gruesome death of Will Scaife. The past few weeks had been a time of tantrums, looks of disgust, and prolonged silences which were becoming ever more difficult to break out of. Reuben and Lizzie would not speak to each other for days on end until something needed attention by both of them, forcing the exchange of the least possible amount of words.

Lizzie felt thoroughly oppressed. No matter how hard she tried, she made no headway. If only she had gone to the farm earlier that fateful day as Reuben had told her to do, things might have been different. She did not need him to keep reminding her of her disobedience. The vision of that half-eaten face and the arm rising so ghostly out of the mud constantly woke her from sleep. All her nightmares were merging into one, with her mother standing on the stairs, surrounded by dancing red and orange flames, pulling the begging hand from the grey squelching mud of the pigsty. Her life was becoming one long nightmare. She thought the best thing to do with Reuben was not to rebel and be drawn into arguments which would end in tears, but just to keep quietly out of his way.

She had taken to visiting Annie, a place which had become a sanctuary during the turbulent times at home. Also having a bad time with the pregnancy, she found solace there in the back room among the bolts of fabrics, but always made sure she was back home in time to prepare the evening meal. The two women had embarked on a heartfelt friendship, whether through pity from Annie or a desperate need from Lizzie didn't matter, it was a friendship which worked. Annie had never taken a positive role in the family before, but someone had to stick up for this young girl if she was not to be controlled by the obstinate Webster brothers. There were often times, though, when Annie was entertaining visitors, that she needed her privacy and Lizzie had soon learned to be discreet.

Annie took it upon herself to talk to Reuben about his sullen attitude and ask why he was being so headstrong. She pointed out that Lizzie, although sometimes needing to be nurtured, was an able young woman if he would just give her the chance. Reuben was not completely heartless. He realised he had not offered Lizzie much of a home, and with a little effort he could make things easier for her. He promised Annie he would give it some thought.

The drovers' road was busy with travellers making their way to market with their mules, sledges, carts or any other adaptable conveyance heavily laden with harvested fruit and vegetables. It was almost Michaelmas Day and sufficient funds had to be raised, by any means possible, to pay their enforced quarterly rents. This was when the exploited workers loyally handed over hard-earned money, swelling the coffers of the already rich landlords.

Inside the forge a horse stood impatiently scraping a loose shoe on the stone-flagged floor. A plough with a broken blade stood in the middle of the floor and a buckled cartwheel was propped up against the wall, all waiting the attention of Jack the blacksmith. Traffic on the drovers' road always brought in plenty of trade for him and today was no exception so Jack was annoyed at the interruption by the unexpected presence of Reuben meddling and getting in his way.

Sparks flew as Jack pumped the bellows until the coals glowed with the required heat to start work. Although the temperature was high inside the forge, the atmosphere was chilly. The two brothers had not worked together since their father had died, but Reuben loved being in the forge, the smell of the hot shoe against a hoof, the heat, working the iron, and the ring of the hammer on the anvil. He was where he belonged. He also missed the bustle of the village and the characters who would stand around the forge, always with a tale to tell. Working up on the moor with his sheep was pleasant enough but very lonely and he was not sure how he would survive the winter up there.

Lizzie had asked Reuben if their old cottage on North Fell could have a new door before the winter set in. A door that would keep out some of the chill and one that she could bolt tight when she needed to feel safe. Reuben had said he would see what he could do and now he was in the forge making the finish of hinges and fasteners to complement his carpentry. The brothers worked round each other in silence. Jack routinely and Reuben delicately fashioning a lock with a distinctive decorative key, unaware that Jack himself had broken the old door down the day he had burst into Townsend Cottage and raped Lizzie.

Jack was agitated, wanting to bring up the subject of the missing deeds, but at the same time not wishing to start a conversation. Twice he had put down his tools and looked at Reuben, but words had failed him. Finally he could not hold back his anger any longer, he had to say something and, slamming his hammer down, he blurted out, 'Damn it. You must know where the deeds to this place are.'

'How the hell should I know where they are?' said Reuben, shrugging his shoulders and showing little interest.

'It would be just like you, ya bugger, to hide 'em.'

'Don't be stupid, why would I do that?'

'To get me thrown out of here, that's why.'

'Just like you threw me out, eh?'

'Yes, you bugger, you'd like to see me lose all this, wouldn't you?'

'Well, then you'd soon find out what it's like to have no work and nowhere to live. Just like I did. I'd like to see how you'd manage.'

'You do know where the deeds are, don't you?'

Reuben did not have the patience to argue with him any more. He tutted and carried on nonchalantly with what he was doing. He was impatient to finish the door and get out of there. Jack's temper slowly festered all morning and he stamped round the forge, muttering under his breath and swearing every time Reuben got in his way. The horse now being shod flinched and struggled at the enraged force of Jack's hammer. Reuben's apathetic attitude provoked Jack until he could stand it no longer and he lunged forward, catching Reuben off guard, hurling him against the wall, and pinning him there with one hand to his throat. A grappling iron hanging from a hook on the wall ripped into Reuben's back, making him immediately arch forward with the pain.

'You bastard, don't play games with me,' Jack snarled.

Reuben instinctively swung his arm round and brought his fist up, catching Jack square in the face with such ferocity that he did not know if the snapping sound was his knuckles or Jack's jaw.

'You lunatic. You know damn well I had nothing to do with all that,' Reuben said, clutching the wound in his back.

Jack, spitting blood, growling and clenching his teeth, grabbed the old cartwheel and slammed it into Reuben's chest, making him reel backwards on to the red-hot coals. He instinctively put his arm out to steady himself, but the sleeve of his jacket caught fire. Entangled in the broken spokes of the wheel Reuben felt the cloth burn the skin on his arm. He plunged his arm into the slack tub, dowsing the flames into a cloud of smoke, the cool water relieving some of the pain. He hurled the wheel back towards Jack, catching him on the side of the head and dropping him to the ground. The startled horse reared up and a hoof landed heavily on the prostrate blacksmith.

'I'll see you burn in Hell,' Jack shouted, rolling quickly from under the frightened animal.

Reuben loaded his finished door on to a cart and made a hasty departure from the forge, over the packhorse bridge, and up the steep hill to Townsend Cottage. There was still enough daylight left to give him time to fit the door in place but his arm was painful and badly blistered. The wound from the hook was open and he could feel blood trickling down his back, but he was determined to get the job finished today. He was making an effort as best he could to redress the contention between himself and Lizzie. She was away for the day, with Annie as chaperone, and the new door complete with lock and key, if in place, he thought, would be a nice surprise for her when she got back.

Annie had fixed up the pony and trap and she and Lizzie had gone to the market, hopefully to sell hats they had made from plaited straw, and make enough money to buy woollen material to make winter dresses. Lizzie was now beginning to fill out and would need a loose-fitting garment for the coming months.

On their return to Dindley they unloaded the parcels from the trap and, while Annie took the packages into her house, Lizzie watered the jaded pony and released it into the paddock at the back of the blacksmith's shop. Jack, who was just finishing off the day and closing up the forge, held the paddock gate open for her, leaving just enough room for her to squeeze back out. He did not speak but his lecherous look warned Lizzie not to linger. As she came close to him she plucked up all her courage and spat straight into his face, then made a hasty sprint down to the bridge. It was such a small gesture in comparison to what he had done to her, but she got great satisfaction from it and, combined with the information she knew about the elusive deeds, she felt reasonably elated.

She trudged up the hill, carrying a large bag of supplies she had bought at the market. It had been a long day, she was weary, and did not feel well. She hated this baby inside her, not only for what it was, but because it was making her feel so ill. The journey to and from the market in Annie's trap had been uncomfortable; she had felt every bump in the rough track and was now glad she was nearly home. The hedgerows either side of the stony lane were heavy with autumn fruits and Lizzie stopped to rest and picked and ate some blackberries and nuts. Two blackbirds also gorging on the fruit were disturbed and darted away but a brave squirrel stood his ground, claiming the hazel nuts as his. It was not until she was nearly at the cottage that she noticed the new door. It looked strong and solid with secure iron hinges and, best of all, she could see it had a lock. She did not go in but stood admiring it for some time; it gave a completely different look to her home. The door was central with a window either side like eyes looking down the valley. She knocked very loudly. Reuben was in the back scullery crouched under the loom, cleaning and repairing it so shouted, 'Come in.' She knocked again.

'Damn it, come in will you?' He threw down his tools and scrambled to his feet to open the door. Lizzie stood there smiling. 'Good day, sir. Have I got the right house? Is this Townsend Cottage by any chance?' she mocked.

Reuben was still angry after his fight with Jack and not in the right mood to join in her fun. He went into a serious, full explanation of how the door operated. Lizzie did not dare tell him that yes, she did know how a door worked, she was just so happy that he had done this for her and kept her, now practised, reserve. He handed her a big key.

'You keep that somewhere safe and use it when I'm not here,' he said.

The key was large and lay across both of Lizzie's outstretched hands. It was shaped like a branch with ivy leaves intertwined round the barrel. She ran her fingers along the metal stems.

'I'll put it in this old candle box and it can sit on the beam above the hearth,' she said.

Lizzie thought this was the most precious thing she had ever been given and, forgetting her sullen behaviour of the past weeks, threw her arms around Reuben. It was then she noticed the fierce burns on his arm and the blood stains on the back of his shirt. He was shaking and there were beads of perspiration on his brow.

Lizzie did not ask how or why and showed no emotion, she just ran out of the door and from the cottage. Reuben's heart sank, just when he needed her she had run scared and left him. He had no idea where she had gone and did not care, he felt so wretched. He thought he would go to bed and try to sleep, hoping the pain would ease and his skin, in time, would heal. He drank a ladle full of water and was about to climb the loft ladder when Lizzie returned, her arms full of greenery. She had been to the meadow and riverside and had searched quickly for special herbs.

She had picked elder, chickweed, coltsfoot, lady's mantle, angelica and willow bark. She chopped, crushed, boiled and mixed some of the herbs with lard until she had washes, poultices, ointments and an infusion. She bathed, soothed and treated Reuben's skin and packed him off to bed with a honey-sweetened herb drink.

'What sort of witch's brew is this? he asked.

'Never mind what it is, just drink it. It'll help you sleep.'

Thunder rumbled round the heavens and lightning lit the cottage that night. Lizzie lay awake in her little alcove bed hoping her witch's brew, which she had rushed to administer to Reuben, would have the right effect. All night she listened to his fevered delirium while the storm seemed to hang overhead far too long. She occupied her mind by counting the seconds between the flashes of lightening and the cracks of thunder, but still jumped when the awaited clap rattled the entire cottage. Reuben slept all the next day and she was frightful that she had given him too large a dose of the potion. She knew well how to mix many concoctions but she was not sure of the potency or how much to render and worried that this would turn into another of her disasters. The hours were endless which she awaited some sign of recuperation. If only she had told Jack about the deeds this would never have happened. She was to blame again. She was down on her knees in desperate prayer when, much to her relief,

Reuben awoke and quietly said that he was much improved.

Over the next few days, Lizzie continued to dispense calming mixtures and anoint him with strange-smelling ointments, the effect of which made Reuben docile and less desperate to get things done. She saw the gentler side of his nature and enjoyed the subdued atmosphere and hoped it would last. Within two weeks his skin was less painful and beginning to heal.

'I'm impressed by your knowledge, Lizzie. How did you know what to do?' Reuben said.

'It tells me in one of my books,' she said sarcastically. 'When I was a child I was burnt very badly and an old lady treated me with her own mixtures. I was interested to learn how she did it so when I found a book in Mr Fothergill's library about herbs and their uses I studied it. I found it fascinating and Mr Fothergill said I could keep the book.' She rummaged under her bed where she kept an assortment of books and trinkets.

'It's here, look.' She showed him a large book with pictures of a variety of plants, some he said he'd never seen before, but Lizzie told him that most grew in the meadow if he took care to look properly.

'Mr Fothergill wrote something on the front page when he gave it to me,' she said, pointing her finger to the inscription and read it to him. 'Nil desperandum. Bruising brings forth the sweetest fragrance.'

'That's nice,' he said, but did not understand a word of it.

'One day I will teach you to read. It's quite easy and you will learn more from books than anywhere else.'

Reuben was not quite sure whether she was right but kept his own counsel.

Their absence from morning service at church for the last three Sundays, due to their quarrels, brought a visit from the rector, his burdened pony laboriously carrying him up the steep lane. They prayed together for Reuben's recovery and for Lizzie's continued health through her term of pregnancy. Then, with two pennies contribution jingling in his pocket, the rector was on his way, leaning back and pulling on the reins as the pony found progressing down the lane a much swifter assignment than the way up.

Annie had been a constant visitor at the cottage during Reuben's convalescence, bringing herbs from her garden which Lizzie had requested. Both her brothers were a great disappointment to her. Trouble in the family always upset her and she was at a loss to know how to rectify the bitter situation.

Even Mrs Dawson arrived at the cottage one day to offer help and advice; her newly born baby strapped to her front in a shawl for easy access to the breast, but on sight of her, Reuben retired to his bed, making it clear she was not welcome. Lizzie was pleased to see her, though, and walked a short way down the lane with her when she left, taking the opportunity to ask questions and allay her fear of the birth of her own baby.

Finally, Bobby Saunders, who had taken up an apprenticeship with the village butcher, came to enquire of Reuben's health since he had not been to the shop with his regular supply of sheep to be slaughtered.

'Hello, Lizzie, you're looking as beautiful as ever and how's the prize fighter?' said Bobby.

'Well enough to go poaching with you, Bobby Boy,' Reuben shouted from the scullery, his high spirits returning.

'A butcher should not need to go poaching,' said Lizzie.

'This one does. I need something to help me pay for my apprenticeship.'

'I haven't had meat for two weeks,' said Reuben. 'I could do with a big fat rabbit in the pot.'

He put on his boots and jacket and set off down the lane, his arm on Bobby's shoulder.

Chapter 17

The farm was starting to generate a small income. Reuben and Lizzie collected heather from the moor which they sold by the cartload to the broom maker, who fashioned and bound it into besoms which he traded around the village and at the markets. Lizzie had acquired, from various sources, some chickens; the rough ground round the cottage being ideal for them to scratch around in. She liked watching them, their feathers shimmering purple, black and green, and the cockerel crowed reliably at dawn. She only used the eggs which they were unable to sell.

Over the past months she had got rid of all the rats, mice, beetles, cockroaches, ants and some unwelcome creatures she could not even name. Worst of all were the fleas, but she had scrubbed and cleaned scrupulously and hoped she had seen the last of them. The meadow was a good source for the plants she needed and, when mixed with ash from the hearth, they made a lye which she used for washing and scouring. Manure from her hens mixed with urine was used for bleaching, but Lizzie could not bring herself to handle this, so collecting and blending this concoction was Reuben's chore.

The cottage was becoming a home, a place more comfortable to live in and now, with a door which closed, Lizzie was able to keep out any unwelcome visitors; animal or human. She still had a problem with the loft ladder but she planned one day to have a sturdy flight of stairs which she could climb with ease. She had so many plans in her head she got quite excited thinking about them and hoped Reuben could be persuaded to be involved in her whims. Since he had become more amiable she was trying very hard not to tip the balance and decided to suggest some of her ideas to him, but she would take her time.

Carding and spinning occupied most of her day, and now the hard work had produced enough yarn for Reuben to start weaving. He sat for hours, the loom clattering away, until the daylight ran out. It was rough cloth but the first roll to come off his loom had been collected and, combined with other weavers' goods, taken by packhorse some distance to a cloth hall in the west of the county and sold to a merchant carpet maker who was interested in buying more. The good news gave Reuben incentive to carry on and he started working into the night by the light of a candle until his arms ached so much that he could no longer move them. Half the value of the cloth was being paid to the carrier and Reuben knew that if he was to make any money from his weaving he would have to buy himself a horse and travel to the markets himself. The price of a horse would take most of his money and he hoped Lizzie would not ask for anything that she needed.

On one of his rare visits to the ale house, Reuben met the new owner of Will Scaife's farm and heard that he had a horse for sale. It was not a strong horse, it had been neglected but, after negotiating what seemed to be a fair price, the poor animal was soon in Reuben's possession. All he needed now was a bridle and reins. He remembered seeing a full harness and wicker panniers hanging up on the wall in the forge. They had not been used for a long time and had established a permanent position behind other broken and rejected implements and were probably destined to hang there forgotten for ever. Reuben would have to swallow his pride if he was going to ask Jack to let him have them. That was easier said than done. His pride would not let him ask, also he was not welcome at the forge so the purchase was going to be difficult but had to be done without delay.

'Good God, I can't believe m' eyes. Come back for another thrashing have you?' said Jack as Reuben walked timidly into the forge.

Reuben did not speak, he just wandered around casually, taking a sly look at the harness and panniers to see what state they were in.

They looked to be in quite good condition. There was some grime where they had been used, and they had gathered dust while they had hung in the forge, but nothing that couldn't be put to rights. And they were just what he needed.

Jack stood, hands on hips, silently watching him. Reuben continued sauntering, a surreptitious smirk on his face. He could see Jack was getting more and more angry, his temper slowly smouldering, and Reuben thought he had better speak before it developed into another fight and he left empty handed.

'I'll give you ten shillings for that old bit of leather up there,' said Reuben, thinking that Jack would tell him he could have it for nothing and to take it out of his way.

'Ten shillings? It's worth more than that,' said Jack.

'No it's not, it's worn out and no good to you.'

'I could get two sovereigns for that.'

'Nobody's going to pay two sovereigns for that piece of old rubbish. Ten shillings, first and final offer.'

'To you I'll reduce it to one sovereign and that's a very generous offer.'

'No, ten shillings. That's all I've got.'

'I'd rather throw the lot in the river than let you have it for ten shillings.'

'Go on then, throw them in the river,' said Reuben, pushing his luck and not expecting him to do it, but Jack grabbed the leather and wicker and marched impetuously across the paddock towards the steep sandy bank. Reuben watched in disbelief as the harness and baskets flew through the air and landed like a cascade in the middle of the fast-flowing water.

'There you are, go fish for the buggers,' Jack shouted in his usual surly manner.

Reuben was furious, such hostility was beyond his comprehension. 'I'll hang for you one of these days, so help me God I will. You're a lunatic, I'm ashamed to call you my brother.'

The water was too deep to wade in to retrieve them and anyway he was not going to give Jack the satisfaction of seeing him frantically splashing about in the river. Turning to walk away he could hear Jack's manic laughter and, looking back, saw him puffing out his chest like a strutting peacock. Reuben could not resist another gibe to ease his annoyance.

'Have you paid your rent yet? Thought you'd have been glad of some extra cash with all that rent to pay,' he shouted, forgetting that when Lizzie had disclosed her secret to him about the whereabouts of the deeds they had agreed not to tell Jack. He had not meant to say anything but was so eager to get his own back, he had blurted it out without thinking.

'What are you talking about?' said Jack.

'The rent. That hundred pounds you owe.'

Reuben continued to walk away but Jack ran after him and grabbed him by the collar, demanding to know what he meant. Jack could tell by the audacious look on Reuben's face that he was holding something back.

'I'll thank you to tell me what you know about it. Come on, you've got to tell me,' said Jack.

He was much taller than Reuben, heavier and rotund, but at that moment he felt very small and vulnerable and knew he was grovelling, which was very much against his nature, but time had run out, payment was due and he was frantic to prove the property was his.

'Why should I tell you, y' swine? You've never shown me any favours. You gave me nothing. You wanted it all for yourself. You didn't give a damn about anybody else's needs. Eight years I've been floundering trying to make my own way. Well, I've made it and now you're the one left with nothing.'

'What do you mean, nothing? It's mine, all this is mine.'

'No, it isn't,' said Reuben with an overwhelming feeling of euphoria at being the one to tell him of his downfall. He stared back at the pathetic figure and waited for some response, but Jack made no answer. The look on his face, his pleading eyes, warned Reuben that to walk away and prolong the agony would be pushing Jack to his limits. He knew how Jack's mind worked. The seething quiet before the wild outburst and lashing out. He could see him growing agitated and there was a point when the teasing had to finish before the provocation ended in disaster, maybe even a fatality.

'Best go see Mr Fothergill. He'll tell you the whole story and what you need to do,' said Reuben, leaving Jack confused and trying to understand how Mr Fothergill could be involved in his dilemma.

Bobby had called in at the cottage, hoping to see Reuben and had been waiting for over an hour for him to return. This meant that Lizzie had been unchaperoned in his company all that time. She enjoyed his now frequent visits and quite liked him, he made her laugh, but she did not take kindly to his familiarity. She was not quite sure which way to take him, whether he was becoming free with his advances or if this was just his jocular way which he had with everyone. She wondered if it would be too presumptuous if she asked him not to call unless Reuben was there. While he waited he had collected water from the beck, lifted the big pan of boiling swill from the hearth and fed it to the pig and chickens, and collected and carried out the ashes. He had done more for her in an hour than Reuben had ever done, but she remembered how nasty Reuben had been when Mrs Dawson had spent the day helping her, telling her the work was for her to do and that she could not have her friends in the cottage.

'Bobby, can I ask you a big favour?'

'Of course. Anything.'

'Don't tell Reuben you've been helping me.'

'Not if you don't want me to. It'll be our secret. Though I can't see what harm it's done,' he said, standing in the doorway between the scullery and the kitchen and being ushered to sit outside at the front door to wait for Reuben, out of her way, the kitchen being the hub of cooking and last minute panic preparing the evening meal.

It was almost dusk; the evening star, rising at the head of the valley, was chasing the setting sun when Reuben returned home disgruntled after the disappointing outcome of his day, his bout of enthusiasm gone and almost ready to give up the struggle.

'Now then, Bobby, what brings you here at this late hour? I can't let your master have any more meat, my ewes are all mated,' said Reuben, feeling burdened by people he could well do without.

'No, I'm not after meat, well not yours anyway. It's bad news I'm afraid,' said Bobby.

'Oh no, I've had enough upsets for one day. I can't take any more.'

'Thought I better let you know that when I was fishing up river today I saw a couple of half-eaten fish on the bank. I think we've got an otter helping himself to our spoils.'

'Right, what are we waiting for? Let's get down there and flush him out. Shut the hens in, Lizzie. He'll have them as well if he's hungry enough.'

They stalked up the river bank and back down a further two miles, but there was no sign of the animal.

'It could be fifteen miles away, they cover a lot of ground looking for the right food,' said Reuben and they both agreed it was a job for Tom the gamekeeper. Then Reuben saw something unfamiliar on the other side of the river. It was quite dark by this time and he could not see clearly.

'What's that over on the other bank under the low branches of that tree?' he asked, squinting trying to make out what it was.

'That's not him, it's just a bit of rubbish that's come down river and got snagged up on something,' said Bobby.

'No, it's not,' said Reuben. 'I recognise that. It's the harness. I can't believe it. I never waited to see if it sank. Jack must have thrown the wicker baskets in first and the leather landed on top of them and it's floated. Bobby, thanks for bringing me down here, you're going to be my best friend for life.'

He forgot about the otter; his concern now was how to get to the other side of the river. He waded into the icy water. It was up to his waist and the current against him was strong, but with Bobby's help he retrieved his prize.

*

Now with a horse of his own and the harness, Reuben was all set up to take his cloth to market himself and reap the full amount from the sale instead of paying a share to the courier. He worked hard, weaving for many hours into the night until the day came when he had produced enough cloth for a full consignment to sell on the next market day. The wicker baskets were shallow and he had calculated that when fitted on the horse they would just clear the parapet of the humpback bridge. They were perfect.

'Tomorrow, Lizzie, I'll set out early and get the merchants' attention before anyone else. Have we got some bread and cheese that I can take with me? And a jar of ale, I don't want to waste time stopping at ale houses.'

'There's just enough left, I think,' said Lizzie.

'It's starting to get dark so I'm going to sneak down the valley to lay some snares then some might be ready to empty by the time I get back from market.'

'Be careful, I don't want you getting caught by the gamekeeper and them big dogs of his. You'll come to a sticky end down there,' she said.

While Reuben was out setting the snares, Lizzie found an old piece of woven cloth and wrapped what little food she could find from their meagre store, ready for Reuben to take with him in the morning. It would have to do until Reuben freed the snares and she could make a big rabbit stew.

A twig snapped under Reuben's foot; the sound emphasized by the lull of the night. He stopped and stood motionless; listening, looking. Something scurried away in front of him, startling him, but he dared not move a muscle. He was used to this fear which gripped the chest, the fear of being caught. There would be no forgiveness for pleading that he was driven by hunger, the punishment would be severe. An owl hooted and another answered the mournful cry like an echo from deep inside the woods. He waited, poised. The moonlight cast dark shadows which took on human form and danced in the breeze like puppets on invisible strings.

When he was sure he was alone, he knelt down and carefully anchored a wire noose. He liked to take his time setting a snare so it would be effective on the first contact. When it was set to his satisfaction he continued on as far as he dared towards the warren, setting more along the way.

He could see the big house in the distance behind the stone wall; the windows, candle lit, shining against the dark sky. Soon the candles would be intermittently blown out as the family retired to bed and the mastiff dogs would be let loose to silently guard the grounds within the walls.

Setting more snares, he left each one in a position where it would not be seen, enabling them to be left unattended for long periods of time with the wire waiting to tighten relentlessly round an unsuspecting creature's neck.

The most successful places to set snares were up against the wall, but this was dangerously near the house. It was getting late and the mastiffs would be out by now. He would have to be quick and a good distance away before the powerful muscular dogs picked up his scent. He bent down near a big base stone to set the last trap. The palms of his hands were sweating and his mouth was dry. He heard the snort of a dog patrolling inside the perimeter wall followed by a deep foreboding bark which would have immediately roused the gamekeeper. Reuben had just seconds to make his getaway. In his haste his foot stepped on a steel trap. The spring triggered the jaws with great force, clamping his leg; the sharp teeth embedding in his skin through to the bone. He tried to pull the jaws apart but the pain was too great. Gritting his teeth he tried again, but his uncontrollable piercing scream betrayed his position.

'Who's there?' yelled the gamekeeper.

Reuben stifled his cry.

'Come on out before I blow your head off.'

'Don't shoot,' pleaded Reuben.

'Got ya. Ya thieving bastard.'

The gamekeeper stood above him, his rifle on his arm; a silhouette against the moonlight. Reuben recognised him and, for self-preservation, quickly made himself known.

'Don't shoot, Tom. It's me, Reuben.'

'I don't care who you are. I should leave you there to rot and let the crows peck your eyes out.'

Tom was well known for protecting his game rigorously and liked to play sadistic games with any perpetrators he caught, whomever they were.

'Well, well,' he mocked, bending down to pull the jaws of the trap open. 'You can take your foot out now. Don't think you've got away with it. I'll give you a ten start to clear off.'

Straight away he started to count. Reuben tried to stand but collapsed in a heap on the ground. He knew Tom would have no qualms about pulling the trigger and he crawled on all fours, dragging his injured leg. He felt every pebble and every twig on the ground under him. He was frantic to get away as fast as he could, but before he could distance himself he heard the count, 'Ten' and the gun went off.

Chapter 18

Lizzie sat up late. She knew something untoward must have happened when Reuben failed to return. He had never taken this long before to lay the snares. She was undecided what to do. If he had been seen and was hiding somewhere he could be there all night afraid to move. She walked round and round the kitchen, and alternated sitting down, standing up, and then looking out of the door to see if she could see him coming up the lane.

The moon was going down but the stars were still bright. A stream of cold air caught her breath and she imagined him out there somewhere shivering. Suddenly startled as an owl swooped down in the beam of light from the open door, she hastily went back inside and walked round the kitchen again. She did not want to be the cause of him being caught; she had to get this right. Another mistake would make her the victim of Reuben's anger yet again. She wished Bobby were here. He would know what to do, where to look.

The candle had nearly burnt out and the chill in the air was filling the room. She poked the fire, trying to get some more life from the dying embers, but got little heat so she snuggled under the covers on her bed for warmth. Lying awake she listened for him, his footsteps, but the only sound was the creak of the old timbers as they cooled. Dawn was breaking when suddenly the door burst open and in the early morning light she saw Reuben on all fours crawling across the floor.

'That no-good bastard shot me,' he said with clenched teeth.

Lizzie helped him on to her alcove bed. He dangled his leg over the side and, too painful to touch, guarded it with cupped hands. In a frenzy of incoherence Lizzie picked out the words he kept repeating. 'He shot me, he shot me.'

She got a knife and slit the blood-stained material of his trouser leg. She reeled back at the sight of the wound; the raw flesh bleeding and the lacerations filled with dirt where Reuben had dragged his leg on the ground. Feeling his pain she wanted to hold him and share it.

'Don't touch my leg,' he said, waving a hand for her to keep away.

'I must. I've got to get the bullet out,' she said.

'No, no bullet.'

'What do you mean, no bullet? You said you'd been shot.'

'Yes, but the bullet whizzed past my head. It didn't hit me.'

He explained how Tom had discovered him at the warren and when he was running to get away he had accidentally stepped on a steel trap. Not one of his own, one set by someone else, he would never set that kind of device. He told her how the claw had sunk into his leg, pinning him down and how Tom had no mercy and had toyed with him.

'I can't believe Tom would do that. Did he mean the bullet to hit you?'

'I really don't know. He could have intended to hit me and missed, or he could have missed purposely just to frighten me. It was dark so his aim might not have been accurate, on the other hand he knew it was me. I don't know. I really don't know. It could have been either. I could hear him laughing, he was enjoying every moment of it. I never did understand that man.'

Reuben winced with pain as Lizzie tried to clean the wound. Applying her ointments had a cooling effect and he started to calm down. He was exhausted after dragging himself all the way home and had gone beyond sleep. His head ached, he could still hear the ringing of the bullet, and the pain in his leg would make sleep impossible anyway. Lizzie soon had one of her sleeping potions ready for him to drink. A strong one to keep him asleep until the pain had eased a little.

The rolls of cloth were still stacked up against the loom ready for market. Reuben would miss the sale now and they really needed the money. Lizzie wondered if she could maybe pack the horse and take the rolls to market herself. She thought Reuben would be so pleased if she took the initiative. He would sleep for the rest of the day and she could be there and back before he woke up. *What a surprise,* she thought, *if I can accomplish this and when he wakes give him the money.* If she could just get one thing right to gain his favour.

It was a damp autumn morning, a mist hanging over the moor was slow to clear. Harnessing the horse was more strenuous than Lizzie had expected. The heavy collar only just scraped over its head and the horse did not take kindly to the unfamiliar handling. It would not stand still, which made the girth strap difficult to fasten. Once the cradle baskets were in place she took the heavy rolls from the scullery one at a time and stacked them vertically. The safest way was to lay them flat but she thought she could pack more if she did it the other way. The baskets were full but there were still two rolls left. Thinking of the extra money they would bring she stacked them on top of the load. Taking the food and drink she had prepared for Reuben she led the packed horse down the lane. The overladen horse, already lame in one leg, limped badly but the downhill slope made the going easier. At the little packhorse bridge the incline of the humpback proved to be too much for the poor beast and it struggled to get a foothold on the moss-covered cobblestones.

'Come on, you lazy good for nothing. We'll never get there at this rate,' said Lizzie, whacking it on the rump. The sharp blow made the horse flinch and, in protest, kick out with its back legs. The front legs splayed from under it. The side baskets banged against the stone parapets of the bridge, dislodging and twisting the horse's girth belt. Lizzie attempted to save the rolls of cloth but the weight knocked her to the ground and they toppled over the side into the river below. The frightened horse bolted and the cloth lay ruined at the bottom of the river. Lizzie sat on the bridge wondering how in heaven she was going to explain this one to Reuben. He had never been violent but he would never forgive her for this and would probably give her a beating.

Lizzie dared not return home and they found her two days later hiding in the old dairy house at Mr Fothergill's house. Reuben could not find it in his heart to forgive and it was well into winter before he even spoke to her and he used the name Numskull to her for a long time.

Winter came early that year with the first fall of snow at the beginning of November and it continued to fall steadily well into December. The otter still ran free and continued to deplete the fish stock as well as the occasional rabbit and duck. Despite the solidarity of the local poachers and many cold nights watching the river bank, they had been unable to track it down. Even Tom the gamekeeper, who had searched with his hounds, had not been able to catch the wily animal. Tom was known to be ruthless when his territory was threatened and was willing to kill anything invading it, saying he had enough trouble with poachers helping themselves to his game without an otter on the scene. Another reason was he would have an excuse to visit Annie if he could cure the skin and take it to her for glove making. Otter-skin gloves were sought after and always brought a profitable price.

Reuben and Lizzie had prepared, as well as they could, for the cold months ahead and all the problems that the bad weather would bring. They had gathered as many twigs and as much bracken as they could find for kindling, as well as broken branches which had been chopped for firewood, and they had stacked it all in a makeshift shelter at the side of the cottage door. A supply of tallow candles made from mutton fat were stored on the kitchen shelf among an assortment of wine, salted meat and pickled vegetables. Lizzie knew it was not enough to last all through the winter months, but it was the most she had been able to deal with. Reuben had such a big appetite and liked to eat big meals. She planned to persuade him to eat less and reduce the expanding bulge of his stomach, but he was not a vain man so she doubted whether he would take any notice of her words.

With each day, silver flakes silently fell and thickened on the ground until one night the wind turned and came from the north. A blizzard raged across the moor, something they had not prepared for. Reuben did not sleep that night; he lay listening anxiously to the wind howling round the cottage and was up and dressed long before the first sign of daylight appeared.

'What are you doing?' Lizzie asked. 'You can't go out in weather like this.'

'I'll have to try and get up on the fell and bring the sheep down if I can. Them drifts'll be so deep I'll have no stock left if I don't. I hope I can find 'em,' said Reuben, looking round for sacking or anything he could strap to his legs for warmth.

'I'll come with you,' Lizzie bravely offered.

'No you won't. Don't be ridiculous. I can't look after the sheep and you as well. You go down into Dindley and see if you can find Bobby Saunders. Knock him up if you have to. Tell him to get himself up here as quickly as he can. He'll need a crook, tell him, and some rope if he has any.'

Lizzie grabbed two shawls, tied one under her ever growing belly for support and threw the other round her head and shoulders. She set off on the trek to the village, leaving Reuben binding his feet and legs with the faulty cloth which had been rejected from his first attempt at weaving. The widest piece he wore as a hood, covering his head and shoulders like a monk at prayer.

Lizzie stumbled as her feet sank deep into the soft snow. Hedge tops had disappeared under deep drifts and she had to trace her way down the lane from memory. Her feet were soon wet and sore and the baby kicked more than usual inside her as if protesting against the cold, an unwanted burden she could have well done without at this time. Having to lift her legs so high out of the snow tired her and she desperately wanted to turn back, but the wind was at her back so she kept going. As she approached the village she was slightly relieved when the sheltered lowland valley path became more defined. It was not yet daylight and cottage windows illuminated intermittently as candles were lit by early risers starting their busy day.

There was no candle burning at the Saunders' family house. Lizzie banged on the door two or three times before she was heard. Mrs Saunders looked down from a window and was some time before recognising the bedraggled snow-clad figure, like an apparition, hunched at her door. Told to wait in the kitchen, the fire not yet lit, Lizzie stood there shivering and rubbing her upper arms with both hands. Bobby was dragged, bleary-eyed, from the warm bed he shared with his two younger brothers. With the promise of sixpence and a bowl of gruel he managed to rouse two other men to join him. They knew they would never get the sixpence but were willing to help.

On the high fells the wrath of the storm had sculpted the snow into drifts deep enough to bury a house and the contours of the landscape were unrecognisable. The four stalwart men worked as a team, keeping together within shouting distance, with Reuben giving instructions on where he remembered the crevices to be and where the deepest drifts might be. The wet flakes cut into their eyes like sharp knives and the wind almost took them off their feet. Their stamina was vital as the icy cold seeped right into their bones, and they no longer had any sensation in their fingers. They sank their crooks up to the curved neck into the drifts, pulling out any sheep they could feel and then guided them down to lower ground. It was nightfall by the time they found the last few sheep. The men trudged back to the cottage, hungry and weary; the challenge had been greater than they had anticipated. Reuben carried a sheep, the heavy weight distributed across his shoulders, the legs girded on his chest.

'That's a dead 'un,' he said, shaking his head in dismay as it rolled down his back landing with a thump on the snow-covered ground at the back of the cottage. Lizzie could see the disappointment in his face and chose to keep quiet and busy herself at her cooking. She had a big pan full of boiled rabbit with barley ready for when they all came in. The men tucked into the food heartily, too tired to notice the unpleasant musty smell wafting round the kitchen as their dirty clothes dried at the big log fire and overpowering the palatable smell of the cooked meat completely.

'One of m' best ewes that was, dead as a doornail, so I've lost the lamb as well, damn it,' said Reuben.

'That's not too bad. It could have been a lot worse if you hadn't been up there so quickly,' said Bobby. The two other men, pushing pieces of bread round their dishes to mop up every last drop of the gravy, nodded in agreement.

'Aye, I suppose you're right. Thanks lads, I'd have still been up there if you hadn't come to help me.'

'I'll come up tomorrow and cut that dead 'un up for you, if ya like,' said Bobby, willing to show off his newly learned skills of butchery. I can get a good price for ya too. Plenty of meat there and it's a good thick skin. She weathered well up on that moor,' he said, putting on his warmed clothing ready for the cold walk home.

'Aye, you do that, lad,' agreed Reuben as he bid them all goodnight.

Reuben retired to bed exhausted and disillusioned, so cold he thought he would never get warm again. His inheritance and the work involved was proving to be more than he could cope with. This was not what he wanted, if only he could go back to the days when he worked alongside his father in the forge. He did not realise at that time what happy days they were. He was a blacksmith not a farmer and he longed to be working in the warm forge again instead of on a freezing bleak moor.

Bobby was true to his word and he arrived the next day with suitable knives and got to work on the carcass. He used the snow at the back of the cottage, now trodden down, as a chopping block and it was stained red when he had finished.

As soon as the ewe had been cut up, Lizzie had the sheep's head boiling away in the big pot on the fire. She was down in the meadow digging up a horseradish root to use for flavouring while the brains, which she had taken out first, were soaking in a basin of salted water on the kitchen table ready to make a sauce. The best cuts of meat and the skin were taken to the village and were soon sold to the big house. Reuben spent the money he was paid on two rows of vegetables in a field on a nearby farm. One row of turnips and one of potatoes which still remained in the ground after the pickers had left and would need lifting without delay.

Chapter 19

By the time the snow began to melt, their meagre food and fuel supplies were almost exhausted and there was no money to replenish them. The snow on the moor had been so heavy that the turbulent melt water was now flowing over the top of the packhorse bridge. The springtime water had risen quickly and gushed down the valley, flooding the meadow which made the track to the village impassable. Reuben was frantic to get his sheep back on to the moor to forage on higher ground and he had left home early that morning without eating or taking food with him to move them.

The last of the logs were burning and cracking on the kitchen fire, the escaping sap hissing like an intimidated goose. The flames lapped round the cooking pot boiling the last turnip. When it had cooked, Lizzie mashed the vegetable in a basin, put a big knob of butter on top, covered it with a cloth, and set off to take it up on to the moor to feed the hungry shepherd.

Waddling like a duck through the sludge and the last of the snow, her loathsome bulge weighing heavily, she climbed the craggy path on to the moor. Resting on the first boulder she came to, she wrapped her cold fingers round the hot basin to keep them warm then lifted the cloth for a peep at the turnip. The smell of the melting butter was too much to bear, especially for someone who had not had any breakfast either, and she could not resist tasting just one spoonful. She savoured the taste as the delicacy melted in her mouth. Feeling very guilty she replaced the cloth and carried on a little further up the track. Stopping to rest again and regain some strength and ease her breathlessness she was so hungry that she thought a second spoonful would not be too much of a sin. The butter had now completely melted and disappeared into the mashed turnip and she had to dig down into the basin for a spoonful that would have the full flavour. She was soon eating a third spoonful and a fourth, there was no stopping now. Reuben saw her in the distance and made his way towards her just in time to hear the spoon scraping the bottom of the basin.

Lizzie had to suffer the wrath of a hungry man for the rest of the day, knowing it was no good arguing. Her excuse was that it was not her fault there was nothing to eat and she insisted it was the Devil himself who had lifted that cloth from the basin. She never could find words ingenious enough to combat his level of provocation and the best course of action was to just keep quiet, as usual.

The day of silence and no communication between them was coming to an end and Lizzie stood at the cottage window, staring aimlessly westward down the valley and wishing she could turn the clock back and return to the security of Mr Fothergill's house. When she thought back to those days she realised she had been happy living there in his service and could not now think why she had wanted to leave. She had never been hungry in those days. There was always food in the pantry and never a day went by without a hot meal served on the table.

By evening the river level was still rising and the setting sun's reflection shimmered on the surface of the water. Fortunately, the cottage was far too high up the fell to be affected by the flood. Lizzie had never seen the sea, she had only read about it in one of her books, but this is what she imagined it would look like.

'Reuben, come here,' she shouted, but he was busy weaving and, because of the clattering of the loom, he was unable to hear her. She had to shout again and reluctantly he broke off from what he was doing.

'Now what?'

'There's something in the river,' she said. 'I think it's a lamb.'

In disbelief he looked out of the window and, sure enough, there was something small and white thrashing about in the water. Maybe it *was* an early lamb.

'You're right for once,' he said and, grabbing a rope, he ran to the edge of the flood with Lizzie following and attempting to keep up with him.

'Where is it? Where's it gone? I can't see it.'

'I can. Right over there,' said Lizzie, pointing and wading into the water.

'Get back, Lizzie. Have a bit of gumption. This is much too dangerous for you,' he snapped.

She felt the fast, cold current of the floodwater lashing round her legs and, unsteady at the thought she might be swept away, made no hesitation in returning to dry land.

'It's not a lamb. It's a dog,' he shouted. He called and whistled for it to come to him but the current was too strong and the dog too tired to swim. The bedraggled animal was washed further downstream before Reuben was able to reach it. He waded into the water and pulled it out on to the grassy edge. It was quivering and gasping for breath. Reuben squeezed its stomach and it vomited a jet of water. He carried it back to the cottage and dried it as best he could, but there was no fire to warm it by. He looked at the poor creature lying on the floor and shivering; a raw gash to one of its legs was bloodied and fierce.

'It looks as if he's been bitten. Could have been after that otter and got swept away by the flood. He's been a grand dog but he's half-drowned. He won't last through the night,' he said.

Lizzie stroked the dog's head gently before covering the wound with some of her ointments, and that night Reuben took the dog into his bed with him to give it some warmth. After two days the dog did start to recover. With the slightest of movement it lifted its head from the bed and slowly looked round at its surroundings. It went straight to Reuben's side and never left it. Everywhere Reuben went the dog followed, whether it was up on the moor with the sheep or poaching up near the big house, and it was not long before it showed a cunning ability to catch a rabbit.

Eventually the floodwater receded. The birds returned and sat along branches in their numbers like beads on a necklace and the noisy caw-caw echoed round the rookery as twigs were rounded into this year's nesting. Buds ready to burst into leaf gave a green haze which graced the trees in the valley bottom. The packhorse bridge was again visible and, after an accumulation of rubbish which had been swept down by the flood had been dislodged from the hump back, it became negotiable once more.

'I'll take the dog down into Dindley and see if he belongs to anyone,' said Reuben, seizing the opportunity to visit the ale house and quench his now overdue thirst.

Wooden beams, grey with cobwebs, supported the low ceiling of the ale house. With the fields not yet spring-dried and it being too wet underfoot to work on the farm, workers had gathered, seated on long wooden settles, in the inglenook and round the room. Their clay pipes, lit with tapers from the big log fire, filled the small room with tobacco fumes while dogs slept contentedly under tables.

The landlord worried that if it did not stop raining soon he would run out of ale; the flagons of cider were already empty. Tom the gamekeeper, not a popular man, sat alone in one corner leaning back, arms folded, listening to the conversations but not joining in. Jack Webster sat among the men and dominated the conversation. Helping himself to ale from a serving jug on the counter he took up position in the middle of the floor and, making sure everyone was listening, continued his tale in his usual callous manner. So intent was his storytelling, willed on by his engrossed audience, that he did not notice Reuben walk in.

'Then, believe it or not, she said she would rather sleep with the old sow so I offered to lead it from the sty, up the stairs, and put it in her bed which, my friends, I am about to do when I leave here,' said Jack, taking another gulp of ale from his tankard. He thumped his fat fist on the nearest table, spilling the contents of tankards which had just been refilled to the brim. There was disbelief at the farfetched tale he had just related, and jeers of denial accompanied the raucous laughter of the men.

'I'll take sixpence from any man who wants to climb my stairs this night and see for himself that my tale is true,' he said, turning round to look for anybody who wanted to take him up on the offer. It was then he saw Reuben standing near the door, a disapproving look on his face, and the conversation dwindled round the room, like an ebbing tide, into hushed silence as the animosity between the two men was recognised.

Reuben's enquiries about the stray dog brought no response. Tom snapped his fingers and the dog went to him and sniffed at his gaitered boots.

'Smell them rabbits, can ya boy?' he said, patting the dog and feeling for a sturdy bone structure. 'Looks like you got yourself a good dog there, Reuben, but be warned, don't you bring him anywhere near the warren or I'll have no hesitation in shooting him. Big shame that would be.'

Reuben, who thought married men should be faithful to their wives, disapproved of the familiarity of the gamekeeper with his sister; nor did he want to appear too friendly with him in front of the other men and he did not answer.

'I'm glad I've seen you. You've saved me a journey. I was just about to ride up North Fell with a message for you,' said Tom.

'Oh, I can't imagine we have any business to discuss,' said Reuben.

'The squire has pledged six militia men by next week to join the ranks of a regiment in the east and you're one of them.'

'No chance. I can't do militia service, I'm much too busy at this time of year, and anyway I'm not in his employ now so he can't call on me,' said Reuben.

'Not a case of can't. You signed up and whatever you think you are now you've still got it to do.'

'But my circumstances have changed since then. I'm busy with the sheep. They're all lambing and I need to be up on the moor all day. And Lizzie's no help, the baby's due anytime. I need to be here.'

Jack Webster sat with a smirk on his face. He couldn't believe his luck. Nothing pleased him more than to see his brother in a fix and he immediately seized the opportunity to turn it to his advantage.

'I'll do your militia duty for you,' he said, laughing. 'You put one hundred pounds in my hand and I'll do it.'

Reuben did not answer, but turned abruptly and left the ale house a despondent man.

Chapter 20

Curled up on her little alcove bed, Lizzie sucked the corner of the blanket, whether consciously or just an automatic reaction, it was something she had not done since she was a small child. The winter dampness had seeped through the roof and walls of the cottage and left an unpleasant fusty smell to the bedding, and it would be a few weeks before the lavender was ripe enough to pick and use to mask the mildewed odour, so the sucking brought little solace to her fretting. She longed to have children one day, but not like this. The traumas just got worse and worse. She felt there would be no end to this nightmare she was living. If God was in his Heaven she wondered how He could do this to her, how many more times He would inflict sorrow upon her, and she prayed that it might stop. Then, in a sudden outburst, she screamed at Reuben more from fear of the unknown rather than temper.

'Militia service? How could you? Am I to be left here on my own? The birth of this baby fills me with dread and the thought of having to endure it on my own mortifies me,' she howled, rolling over to face the wall.

Reuben, feeling a twinge of compassion, put his arms around her and pulled her towards him, but she felt no affection towards him whatsoever and pushed him away.

'Why, why did you enrol? Tell me why? You idiot, you didn't have to.'

He shook her to stop the hysterics and to make her listen. He put both hands on her shoulders and looked straight into her sorrowful eyes, so blue against her black tangled hair.

'Yes, I did need to enrol. It was a condition of my employment with the squire. You know, I've told you often enough that it was the only job I could get when Dad died and Jack took over as blacksmith and threw me out of the forge. The squire would only take on men who were willing to fight when called upon. If he could allocate enough men it was good for his reputation and a boost to his importance among the nobs. Militia service didn't mean a thing to me at the time. I never thought I'd ever be called upon. I was desperate. I would have agreed to anything to get work and somewhere decent to live. You have no idea how horrible the hiring markets are. Stood in a line with unscrupulous employers sneering at you, examining your teeth, and asking you to undress so they can see if you're clean and if you have any muscles. It was degrading.'

Lizzie, pushing Reuben's hands from her shoulders, the corners of her mouth firmly set in a silent sulk, started to busy herself around the kitchen, although pottering at nothing of purpose.

'Anyway, the baby isn't due for another month. It's the sheep and lambs that'll need looking after. I'll probably be back long before the baby arrives,' said Reuben, tactlessly trying to justify himself; although, not knowing the true date, that was the worst statement he could have made.

'Babies come when they're ready. Sometimes early,' Lizzie said, trying to lay the foundations for the birth which she knew was imminent.

'I'll ask Bobby to go on the moor and check the sheep as often as he can while I'm away and maybe you'd be happier if Annie stayed here with you.'

'I can't see Annie sleeping in a pitiable place like this, anyway she has her business to run and knows absolutely nothing about babies, nor does she care to know.'

'There is one way I could get out of it, if I paid someone to do the service for me. Jack said he would do it if I paid him one hundred pounds, but of course we have no money. Where would I get that sort of money?'

'You could borrow it,' Lizzie suggested, trying to be practical for her own sake, but the idea that they should give money to Jack to pay his rent infuriated her. This man would have power over her once more, again he would have the upper hand. With clenched teeth she was on the verge of blurting out her secret and breaking her promise to Annie not to tell him of the trauma that Jack had inflicted on her. Fortunately Reuben interrupted her just in time.

'Don't you think I have enough problems without debt hanging round my neck? No, I must go and do the service I'm expected to do.'

Lizzie, exasperated and with no other solution to the problem, returned to the confines of her bed to sulk in peace. The next day she visited her confidante, Annie, who listened sympathetically but, with no desire to get involved in the insolvent couple's finances, suggested it was a matter for Mr Fothergill and that Lizzie should go to seek his advice. This seemed to be a good idea and maybe the solution, so Lizzie thought she might do that. He would be sure to help her.

Lizzie sat in the parlour on the edge of a high-backed wooden chair strategically placed in front of the desk. She knew that calling to see Mr Fothergill would be very much against Reuben's wishes, which made her rather nervous for fear she should say the wrong thing. She had to get this right. Ever since she had come to live in this house six years ago she had thought of it as her home and she had been able to confide in Mr Fothergill as a father figure, but now she was married she realised the relationship was different, more business-like. He was seated behind his large desk writing, dressed in a scarlet waistcoat buttoned over a rather grubby shirt, the pen scratching across the paper.

'Sorry to interrupt your train of thought, Mr Fothergill, but I have an urgent matter to discuss with you,' she said, trying to sound business-like and introduce her new position of importance.

'Another book, as you can see. I am very eager to finish it,' he said without looking up and continued to write, stopping only to flick through pages of reference books and diaries, his fat red cheeks puffing and deflating after each laboured exhalation.

She sat quietly, waiting for him to finish, and felt as if she was almost invisible to him, but then she had walked in without knocking. Her idle fingers picked dust from the carving on the wooden arms of the chair and, looking round the room, she thought how dishevelled it had become. There had never been such dust when she lived there, she would have regularly polished the furniture with beeswax, perfumed with lavender, and Mr Fothergill would never have worn a dirty shirt.

Portraits of Mr Fothergill's ancestors, still in the same prominent positions on the walls, looked down on her as if they were judging her every move. Goodness only knew what the library would be like, where Lizzie used to dust for hours just for the opportunity to read the books.

She had prepared her story in her mind, how Reuben was working so hard and the money was vital for him to succeed. No way must she say it was for her own preservation. Mr Fothergill was a single man and would not understand the feelings of a woman, especially one about to give birth. Through the night she had tossed and turned, getting no sleep as she rehearsed every word. Earlier, walking across the fields towards the house, she had rehearsed yet again and had been word perfect; but now, pompously being kept waiting to deliver the practised speech, she felt it fading away as trivial compared to the publication of an esteemed book.

Some of the books that Lizzie had read related to his travels. When he was a younger man he had crossed the sea to foreign lands and seen sights she could only dream about. He had written about great palaces, cathedrals with gigantic painted walls and ceilings, and mountains with smoke coming out of the top. There were tales of emperors, kings, monks and scavengers, battles fought on land and at sea, fortunes made and lost, and flamboyant clothes the likes of which would never be seen in Dindley village. More recently he had taken an interest in plants and his books were now catalogues of exotic flowers he had collected. Lizzie was eager to know what this latest book was about and walked round the desk to peep over his shoulder, which brought an immediate guarded reaction.

'Could you go to the kitchen and make tea for us while I continue? You know where everything is,' he said, abruptly stretching his arm to the ink well and discreetly hiding the page.

Returning from the kitchen with a tray of tea some minutes later, she asked, 'Where's your butler? I couldn't find any cake.'

'He's unwell and has taken to his bed.'

'No work has been done and you're lacking stores in the pantry.'

'As I said, he is ill and I fear for his recovery. I myself prepare him light suppers but he doesn't eat them.'

'What did the physician say?'

'That it is a consequence of his lifestyle and all he can do is take the laudanum and maybe a little honey, but it does little to ease his pain.'

Not sure what the butler's lifestyle was, Lizzie offered to bring some of her own cures for him, cures that were becoming known and popular with the villagers and which had raised an odd penny or tuppence for her, but he dismissed her suggestion out of hand, knowing nothing more could be done.

'Maybe I could call on Mrs Dawson and ask her to visit and help you.'

'No, don't do that. She brings so many of her children with her and I cannot work with small children caterwauling and running around, and besides they do so pilfer the pantry.'

'Well, they won't pilfer it now, there's hardly anything in there,' said Lizzie.

This was not getting to the object of her visit and she found it hard to change the subject to her problems, but change it she must without delay. It was now late into the afternoon and almost time for her to return home. When the tea was drunk, Lizzie began to tidy the cups and plates back on to the tray and begin her tale of woe, feeling it would be easier if she walked round the room as she spoke and did not have to look him straight in the eye. Sitting back on the chair when her story was done she waited for his answer.

'That is a lot of money, Lizzie. How do you propose to repay me?' he asked, tapping his fingers on the desk, his head to one side, and a quizzical look on his face.

Lizzie, in her haste, had not thought as far ahead as paying back and spluttered unrehearsed words about lambs being sold and fleeces and woven cloth going to the wool market.

'I think you had better ask Reuben to come to see me. This is a matter I need to discuss with him. Must get on,' he said, pulling on the bottom of his waistcoat and picking up his pen, leaving Lizzie in no doubt it was time for her to leave.

She had hoped to return home with a deal all sealed and complete and proudly present the money to Reuben. Without this success she knew she should not have interfered, this was men's business, so to keep the peace she did not even tell him she had been to see Mr Fothergill.

Within the week, Reuben had been rigged out in a makeshift uniform, mounted on horseback, and had set out to join a regiment on the east coast.

Chapter 21

At the Saunders' house a garland of flowers lay on the kitchen table. Cowslips and bluebells, picked from the woods, had been delicately entwined round a ring of apple blossom. A white satin dress and a blue sash were neatly draped over the back of a chair. Lucy, Bobby's sister, had been up since dawn, too excited to sleep for today she was to be crowned Queen of the May. She had dreamt of this day as long as she could remember and had waited so long to be twelve years old, the age required for this fairy-tale honour.

In the centre of the village the maypole stood proud, topped with a weathervane, the arrow dithering on its axis between the direction of a freshening wind and driving rain. Lucy prayed for the rain to stop but the rumble of thunder in the distance gave her little hope. The wind strengthened as the full force of the storm approached the village from the direction of North Fell. Thunder rattled the windows and shutters, and lightning lit up the room. After the storm had passed over, the wind reached gale force and the rain continued as if it would never end.

Lucy sobbed as she thought the ceremony might not go ahead and she would not be crowned. Next year she would be too old, this was her only chance and it looked as if it was to be denied her.

'There, there. Take heart, Lucy,' said Mrs Saunders. 'If you don't stop crying you'll have red water-gall eyes and then if the gala does go ahead you won't look very pretty.'

Lucy tried her best to shape her lips into a smile but the tears would not stop and Bobby did not help when he returned from the village, the bearer of bad news.

'There'll be no dancing quickly round the maypole today. It's much too windy to release the ribbons,' he said, taking off his jacket and shaking off the rain. 'The fiddler's gone home and the chimney sweep hasn't even bothered to turn up. The morris dancers are in the alehouse and soon they'll all be too drunk to stand up, never mind dance.'

Lucy looked at the garland of flowers. She had searched the fields and woods and found the best blooms in a dell at the head of the river. She had arranged them and tied them up with blue ribbon which matched the sash and then rearranged them until she was satisfied they looked perfect but, like her dreams, they were now starting to wilt.

'I best get up to North Fell. I promised Reuben I'd check on the newborn lambs. They'll be none too happy in this wet weather,' said Bobby, glad of an excuse to leave the women to their woeful whimpering.

It was still raining hard as Bobby trudged up the lane towards the moor. Black clouds floated across the sky and all the birds had gone to ground. Leaning into the strong wind, he jumped the deepest of the puddles but turned quickly when he thought he heard someone shouting. The noise of the wind and rain was deceptive and maybe he was mistaken. It was not the sort of weather for anyone to be outside so far from the village, but he listened for a while and heard it again over in the direction of the meadow. Curiosity urged him to investigate and he found a gap in the hedge where he could push through. He saw someone lying on the wet grass in the shelter of a clump of shrubs. As he approached he was shocked to find Lizzie in a very distressed state.

'Are you out of your mind? What on earth are you doing out here?' he asked, kneeling down to help her up on to her feet.

'Oh. Bobby, I'm so relieved to see you. I need help. Do something. Get someone, quick. The baby's coming.'

'How long have you been here?'

'The pain started at nightfall. I was frightened on my own so I set out to get help. But the pain became too bad and I could go no further. I've been here all night. The dog stayed by my side and kept me warm but as soon as the thunder started he ran off.'

'You're soaked to the skin. Here, let me carry you back home.'

Lizzie, cold and trembling, put her arm round his neck and together they struggled across the meadow and up the lane back to the cottage. While she changed into dry clothes he politely turned round and stared at the wall, shuffling uncomfortably in this unfamiliar situation and at a loss as to what to do next. He remembered six years ago when his sister was being born, and how he was sent out of the house for the day and warned not to come back until he was told. Now he wanted to do the same and just get out of there.

'This is nothing I'm able to deal with, Lizzie. I'll go and get some help from the village.'

'No, don't leave me. Please, Bobby, don't leave me. I'm so frightened and the pain is so bad,' she said, grabbing hold of his arm to keep him there.

The look of pain on her face upset him. He did not want to appear insensitive but this was no place for him, this was woman's work. He kissed her compassionately on the forehead and quickly made his way to the door.

'I'll be as quick as I can, I promise.'

As he ran from the cottage she was still screaming for him not to leave her. He hesitated, wondering if he should stay with her, but then decided he would definitely be better getting help from someone more qualified.

'Mam, Mam,' Bobby shouted, bursting through the door flustered and out of breath after running all the way home. He could hardly get the words out to tell her what was wrong. 'It's Lizzie. Lizzie, she needs someone up there with her. The baby. The baby, it's coming and she's on her own. Can you go?'

'Go and tell Mrs Dawson, she's the best one in these matters. She's delivered more babies than I'll ever see. Tell her I'll be across soon and I'll see to her brood. They'll all be shut inside this weather, not running wild as usual, so I won't have to go looking for 'em.'

It was late evening before Mrs Dawson organised herself for the long walk through the unrelenting rain to Townsend Cottage. She had been baking bread to sell in the village and could not leave it unfinished. The pretentious doctors' portmanteau, which she took with her on these occasions, was filled with improvised gadgetry that she might or might not need. It was heavy and she passed it from one hand to the other as she trudged up the steep lane. Having attended so many births and also having six children of her own, the self-elected midwife had no time for dramatics and liked to just get on with the procedure, take her money, and go. By the time she reached the cottage she was out of breath and short-tempered. Putting her shawl to dry she needed to sit on a chair to rest for a little while before assisting with the birth.

Lizzie was now beside herself, delirious, writhing on her little alcove bed, all sense of reality gone and genuinely thinking she was about to meet her maker. The pain had lasted such a long time that she was moaning and groaning and shouting incoherently and so loudly that she did not hear Mrs Dawson arrive.

'Jack Webster, the Devil surely put you on this earth. Why did you choose me? I didn't deserve this. Curses on you, Jack Webster, you're evil, I hate you, may you rot in Hell for eternity.'

Lizzie's frenzied shouts had Mrs Dawson, with her head on one side straining to listen, trying to make sense of what she was hearing. *What on earth had Jack Webster to do with all this?* There could only be one solution to words like that and Mrs Dawson was the right person to assemble such shocking rantings. This would surely go to the top of the list of putative fathers in her portfolio of gossip. She could only speculate what had been going on and the re-telling no doubt would be an imagined fabrication.

She pushed everything on the kitchen table to one side to make room for her big bag. Tipping it up, gruesome instruments and bottles splayed out on to the wooden surface with a clatter. Lizzie sat up immediately at the noise and saw the array of tools and Mrs Dawson, like a witch, sorting through them. She curled up tight fearing what was going to happen to her.

'Here, have a swig of this,' Mrs Dawson said, passing a small flagon to her. 'It'll help ease the pain.'

'What is it?'

'I've no idea, but it works.'

Glad of anything that would relieve the agony Lizzie downed the lot, coughing and choking as the liquor caught the back of her throat and burned all the way down into her stomach.

'Right, let's have a look at you, young lady. We need to get that baby out of there.'

Lizzie looked again at the assortment of tools on the table, some she had seen Reuben use on the sheep in a brutish way with no consideration for the feelings of the sheep.

'Don't you dare touch me,' she screamed, determined none of that ironmongery was going to be used on her.

'Nonsense, child. We don't want a dead baby, do we now? We want a nice healthy bairn to show to Reuben when he returns home.'

Slowly Lizzie relented, lifting her dress just to her knees. Mrs Dawson put her hands under the skirt and prodded and poked Lizzie's swollen belly. Lizzie did not welcome the intrusion and squirmed and wriggled uncomfortably.

'Keep still, Lizzie, I can't find where the baby's head is.'

On examination Mrs Dawson realised that the baby was in the dangerous breech position and she would have to try to turn it the other way up. She decided not to explain the procedure to Lizzie who was exhausted, and by now quite intoxicated from drinking the firewater and in no state to understand what was happening to her anyway. All through the night she leant over Lizzie and gently massaged her belly until her arms ached and she was too weary to do more. It was enough, the baby successfully turned and made its entrance into the world heralded by the birds singing the dawn chorus.

'It's a boy, Lizzie. Look at him, Lizzie,' Mrs Dawson announced, excitedly happy that her hard work was successfully finished and she could return home, but Lizzie just buried her face in the pillow with no desire to look. She did not feel any of the joy that a firstborn should bring, she was just glad it was all over. For two days and two nights she had suffered the pain of this demon that had been inside her, and now she was free of it she wanted no more attachment to it. She had never felt so tired and had no problem sinking into a deep sleep. Mrs Dawson wrapped the baby tightly in a sheet, covered completely like a cocoon, and laid him on the bed at Lizzie's side. Just as she was packing all her paraphernalia back into the big bag, Annie arrived enquiring as to the welfare of the baby.

'I came as soon as I heard,' she said.

Mrs Dawson took her to one side and, speaking in a whisper, asked, 'Annie, are you able to stay here with Lizzie for a while? She's very pale and will need time to regain her strength.'

'Yes, of course. For a short while anyway.'

'She will sleep as long as the baby does but when he wakes she'll need someone here with her.'

'Don't worry, I'll be here. I'll see to her.'

'She was so tired she wouldn't even look at the baby and when she does see him, it'll more than likely be a shock to her.'

'Of course it won't be a shock. Whatever gave you that idea?' said Annie, cutting her short and thinking what a stupid remark from this foolish woman. She did not pursue the remark further and busied herself round the cottage. Mrs Dawson followed her round to make sure she had understood what she was saying.

'She will need help with feeding, there may be a problem,' said Mrs Dawson.

'Stop fussing. I'm sure Lizzie will cope well enough,' said Annie, helping to lift the bag from the table and almost pushing her out of the door.

'Hmm, we'll see about that. I pray you're right. I can't stop any longer, I have the bread to bake. I'll be back later for my money. I worked all through the night, I might tell you.'

Chapter 22

As the newly born entered the world in the early hours, so the ulcered body of Mr Fothergill's butler was laid out and prepared ready to leave it. The nurse, who had been in attendance for the past month, was paid and thanked for her loyal and discreet care during the unpleasant syphilitic illness.

The parlour curtains, respectfully drawn, made the room gloomy and the Reverend Augustus Sewell struggled to get his sunken eyes used to the dim light by adjusting his spectacles at different positions on his long nose. The top of the large desk had been cleared of writing materials and the open coffin lay unceremoniously across it. The shroud covered only the body of the corpse leaving the face with eyes, being too swollen to be closed, staring inertly at the ceiling.

Standing beside the open coffin, the rector felt distinctly nauseous. He dug deep into his sleeve and brought out a lace-trimmed handkerchief, blessed it, flicked it open and spread it over the grey pustular face of the deceased. Now that the body was totally covered and less offensive, he muttered a quick prayer and a loud relieved, 'Amen,' and stepped away to confer with Mr Fothergill.

Speaking in a whisper, as if the dead might be able to hear what his forthcoming fate was to be, Mr Fothergill gave precise instructions. 'It's to be a quiet and prompt funeral, within this very day. No unnecessary formality and definitely no mourners.'

'Fear not, my friend. The church will be empty apart from you and myself.'

'No, no, no,' he said, wagging his finger to emphasize his request. 'You don't understand. I won't be there. I can't risk being seen to show any outward sign of emotion.'

'I beseech you to reconsider such a rash decision, out of respect if nothing else.'

'You alone, Rector, know that he was more than a servant. He was very dear to me and brought joy and intimacy into my life. My loss is so great I would not be able to contain my grief and it would clearly be detected as distasteful in the eyes of others,' he said, determined to take action that would guard any sign which might diminish his assumed decorum.

The rector, although startled by such authority and immediacy at such a grievous time, knew he would be well rewarded if the instructions were instituted exactly as demanded, and with the church coffers at the usual low ebb he was prepared to oblige. Mr Fothergill had been generous in the past and he saw no reason why he would not be again.

'I'll see to your requests without delay,' he promised, but secretly he was not quite sure if this could really be undertaken within the day. The part-time grave digger and the pole bearers would all have to be found and taken from their normal day's work at short notice.

Mr Fothergill walked over to the open coffin and placed his hand on the butler's shoulder. There was a moment of silence while he reflected on happier times. Their radicalism, which had brought them together at university. How they had been going to change the world, but as the years went by they had mellowed and hidden from the publicity so that their friendship could be fulfilled. He said a quiet goodbye with a kiss to the cold fingertips and slowly closed the coffin lid.

'I did all I could while he was alive, there's no more I can do now. My trunk is packed for travelling and stands waiting in the hallway. A carriage will be here shortly to take me to Hull.'

'Then what are your plans, may I ask?'

'I'll take the continental tour. Maybe, if the good Lord permits me, I'll reach Italy, wallow in the art treasures of the world, sit in the sun, and converse with like-minded people. Maybe I shall learn to play the new card game of solitaire. I will return home only when I'm fully recovered and relieved of my grief.'

'With your permission, I'll arrange contact with suitable clergy who will listen to your prayers, give you guidance, and pass you on to others in whichever country you visit.'

'Thank you. I will be glad of that. May I ask you, you being a man of eminence, to deal with my affairs while I am gone?'

'Of course. I will help you every opportunity I get.'

'Good. Please feel free to use my library. Consult with my solicitors if there is anything you are unable to administer,' he said, completely in control of the situation, although saddened; there was a total loss of his usual sprightliness as he moved around the room.

'I pray that the time will not be too far distant until God grants you peace of mind, and you return to us safely.'

'Thank you, my blessing upon you. I will write often. Just one more thing. It's about Lizzie. Even though she's a married woman I still think of her as my ward. She has many burdens in her life and can at times be very impetuous. Will you see that she looks well into her Bible and receives your Christian guidance?'

'I will do my best. I'll be seeing her after the baby is born to give the Thanksgiving of Childbirth and I will have a long talk to her then. Goodbye. I wish you a safe passage and may God be with you, bless you and keep you,' the rector said, then straddled his faithful steed and trotted away.

When the carriage arrived Mr Fothergill boarded very quickly, bidding farewell to no one, and left without knowing that Lizzie had been safely delivered of a son.

While Lizzie slept a deep, intoxicated sleep, the baby lying beside her, Annie found work which needed attention and made herself busy around the cottage in her usual matter-of-fact manner. First she snuffed out the candles, which were now down to stubs after burning all through the long night. In the scullery she squeezed passed the loom, which still had a half-woven piece stretched across the frame, just as Reuben had left it. She admired the cloth and how Reuben had advanced with his weaving, now entwining coloured threads.

Filling the stone laundry boiler to the brim with water, she struggled with kindling, unable to get the fire to light underneath. The flint was damp and would not spark, but eventually she had the fire roaring away. It had taken four journeys to the beck carrying the water in a leather bucket before the boiler was full. Fortunately the rain had stopped, but she was not happy about her wet, muddy boots obtained in the process. She looked in the pantry for food, thinking that it must have been at least a full day and night since Lizzie had eaten and she would be ravenous when she woke, but all she could find was milk and a little bread.

As soon as she heard the baby whimper, she heated the milk and mixed in the bread; the pobs would be nourishment enough for Lizzie for the time being. The whimper soon became a loud cry and Lizzie rolled over, away from the baby, and buried her face in the pillow, pulling it round over her ears.

'Let's have a look at him then,' said Annie excitedly.

Lizzie's muffled voice from the confines of the pillow demanded he be taken away, and she made it clear that she was not ever going to look at him. The only person she wanted to see right now was her mother. Someone who she missed so much, someone who always soothed and cured and solved all her childish problems, but this was not infantile. Those days were long gone and Lizzie felt that this situation she had got herself into now was more than she could cope with. She felt so miserable she just wanted everyone and everything to disappear.

'Come on, Lizzie, don't be silly. He needs feeding before he bawls the roof off.'

Annie picked the bundle up from the bed and, with a delighted curiosity, pulled the cover away from his face. By now the sun was up and lit the room. Startled by the sudden exposure to the bright light, the baby's tiny eyes blinked and tightened and his crying was suddenly silenced by the unexpected movement. Annie stared silently at the harsh features. The face and head were cut and bruised where Mrs Gates had used her instruments in haste, but the ugliness was intensified by a cleft lip cutting deep into the mouth. The brief smile gone from her face, she was unable to speak. There were no spoken words that could describe how saddened she was, and she wondered how much more Lizzie would be able to take. Sensing the momentary silence, Lizzie quickly swung round and sat up on the bed.

'What is it?' she asked.

'Nothing, he's lovely,' said Annie, trying to push him on to Lizzie's breast to be fed without her seeing his face, but Lizzie saw that her smile had gone and snatched the blanket away from the baby.

'Oh, my God. Get rid of him,' Lizzie said, pushing him back into Annie's arms.

'Don't talk nonsense.'

'Give him away. Do what you like with him. I don't want him.'

'Oh, for heaven's sake, Lizzie, he's your son. Poor little soul, it's not his fault how he came to be. He depends on you and will do so for many years. You'll grow to love him in time.'

'Never. Wild horses wouldn't get me to touch him. Look at him. He's got the sign of the Devil engraved all over his face.'

The baby howled, demanding attention as the breast was denied him. Annie, anxious to return to her home and her own work, was becoming impatient and shouted at Lizzie above the noise.

'And what will Reuben think when he gets back home and the baby's not here, given away to goodness knows who? You'll give the game away acting like this. You've got to keep pretending, he must never guess our secret.'

Annie and Lizzie both looked up, alarmed to see Mrs Dawson standing in the doorway. Expecting there to be problems, she had called early for her money hoping she could be of further assistance and that there would be an opportunity for more money to be made. They had been so boisterous with their disagreement they had not heard her arrive and hoped she had not overheard, but she had heard it all. The argument and the bitter remarks just went to confirm her suspicions and add to her stash of gossip.

'Well, there's nowt wrong with his lungs. What seems to be the problem?' she asked.

'I don't know, I just don't know. Lizzie seems to be just too tired to feed him. She's still recovering from her ordeal and whatever it was you gave her to drink.'

'It was just a drop of wine I make myself. I've used it dozens of times and been complimented on how soothing it is. She'll soon sleep it off and be none the worse for it.'

'I hope so. In the meantime can you do anything to stop this babe from crying?'

'Here, give him to me, though I doubt if he'll feed easy,' said Mrs Dawson, discarding her shawl. The infant nuzzled up to her and she attempted to nurse him against her own breast, turning him to different angles but without much success.

'No, it's no good, he's not able to suckle. He's trying, bless him, but his lips can't grasp,' said Mrs Dawson, putting her finger into the baby's mouth to temporarily appease his crying.

'What do we do now then?' asked Annie.

'There's only one thing for it. Go outside to the byre and find the thickest piece of straw you can and bring it to me. Quickly now.'

Annie, not used to being ordered about, was a bit taken aback but realised she was at a total loss in such circumstances and was in no position to argue. Not understanding what Mrs Dawson was going to do, but sensing the urgency, she soon returned from the byre with a bunch of straw for her. She watched silently as Mrs Dawson took a stalk from the bunch, washed it, filled it with her own milk, then put it deep into the baby's mouth. He didn't like it and tried to cough it out but it was far enough into his mouth that the milk ran down his throat. She repeated this time-consuming task over and over until the baby was satisfied and he fell asleep.

'There now. That's what you must do. It'll take a long time and a lot of patience, but it's the only way, and between you both it should not be too great a burden. Would you like me to call later in the week to see how you're getting on?'

'No thank you, Mrs Dawson. I'm sure Lizzie will manage.'

With a loud, doubtful huff she left the cottage and, heading for the lane, shouted without turning round, 'And I still haven't been paid.'

Chapter 23

'Mark my word, Son. There'll be trouble up there before long. You'd do well to keep away.'

Mrs Saunders bent over the big flat pan, the fire lashing the sides, frying bacon freshly cut from the ham. The aroma filled the kitchen. Four hungry faces sat round the large table all waiting for their breakfast before starting the day.

'But Mam, I promised Reuben I'd look in on Lizzie. I haven't been for two days and she's up there on her own without any food,' said Bobby.

'And whose fault's that? She knew what was ahead. She should've prepared for it.'

'Ah, well, it all happened before it should have,' Bobby said.

'Not according to what folk round here are saying, it didn't.'

'Oh Mam, it's all tittle-tattle. It's a pity folk haven't got anything better to talk about. I've got to go, I promised I'd look after the animals as well. Anyway, Mrs Dawson has given me some bread to take up to the cottage for Lizzie.'

'Oh, in that case, take a pot of that honey off yon larder shelf and there's a fresh pail of milk outside she can have,' said Mrs Saunders, not wanting to be outdone by a loaf of bread.

'Thanks, Mam. I'll be back in time for m' dinner.'

'Aye, see that you are, Son, don't be hanging about up there or they'll be talking about you next.'

Bobby was given various offerings as he walked through the village and ended up with quite a load to carry up the lane to Townsend Cottage. Despite family feuds and fierce rivalry within the village, the women would put aside their quarrelling and pull together in times of hardship; unlike their obstinate men who would sit in the inn unable to openly admit when they were struggling and wanting. Whether it was food, fuel, clothes, money or child minding there would be sharing or handing down or looking after; the women would help each other. Even Lizzie, not being related to anybody in this close-bred community, and who had been considered an outsider, was now included in these charitable acts.

It was a bright May morning, calm after the storm. Not yet summer temperatures but pleasant. The river had receded back to the natural tree-lined banks and the leaves, newly opened, were at their greenest, the time of year Bobby like best. Halfway up the lane he unloaded the gifts and, with one big sigh, he sat and rested for a while. The heavy rain had freshened the land and an earthy smell rose from the ground. Throwing his head back he took a long, deep breath and filled his lungs with the invigorating air.

He watched the birds. Some already feeding their young, some still fighting over nesting sites. He could hear the forlorn cry of the curlew away in the distance on the moor and the bleating of lambs. The noisy rookery in the tallest of the ancient trees on the edge of the meadow added notes, all blending together like an orchestra tuning up before a big overture. An eagle soared high above the moor and then was soon out of sight as it flew towards the distant fells. There was a good view of the valley from this point. The forge and paddock; the inn; the church, its solid tower outlined by the sun directly behind it; the row of workers cottages; and at the far end his own family home and the river like a crumpled ribbon joining them all together.

He could have enjoyed the walk if he had not been laden with so much to carry, but persevered as he anticipated the look of delight on Lizzie's face when he walked in to rescue her once again. He thought of himself caring more and more for her and she increasingly relying on him, but he must put such thoughts out of his head because soon Reuben would be back home and then all would return to normal with Lizzie happy and busy with her newborn baby.

The dog barked as Bobby approached the cottage and woke Lizzie from a much needed sleep. A bang on the door simultaneously as it opened did not give her time to rise. He found her lying on top of the covers on the little alcove bed, her black hair, with a sheen of blue where a beam of sunlight from the open door caught it, spread out on the pillow. She was calm now, so different from the day he had left her thrashing about in pain, but he could not understand why she was fully clothed and her shoes were damp. He put it out of his mind as she looked up and welcomed him with a sleepy smile. She rested on her elbow as he showed her the gifts telling her who each one was from.

'I can't cook, Lizzie, but I'll cut you some bread and cheese if you like.'

The dog followed his every step, frantically yapping at his ankles.

'What's the matter with you, boy? I've nothing for you to eat. Go on get out, go find yourself a rabbit,' he said, pushing it out of the door. He watched as it bolted round the back of the cottage and up the track, heading straight for the moor.

'That dog's missing Reuben. He's gone looking for him,' Bobby said.

He cut a thick slice of bread and broke the cheese. He poured some milk into the cup. As he handed it to Lizzie, he pondered again on the damp shoes. She should not have been out of bed but maybe she had been down the garden to the privy or just needed some fresh air, and he soon dismissed it from his mind.

'Here you are. Eat that. Then I'll go outside and see to the livestock. I expect you'll be wanting to feed the baby. I've not seen him yet. Where is this son of yours, where have you hidden him?' he said.

She licked her dry lips and ate quickly and greedily, talking excitedly at the same time so that Bobby could not understand what she was saying.

'Wow, slow down, you'll choke.'

'I'm so happy, Bobby. Don't you see? It's all over. At last I can start again and not make the same mistakes.'

'What do you mean?'

'I can put all this behind me. I don't need to live here anymore. As soon as I can get out of this bed I want to go back to Mr Fothergill's. Like it used to be.'

'You can't, he's not there. He's gone away. For a long time I believe. All the windows are shuttered, the doors are latched, and he's cancelled his meat order for the foreseeable future.'

'What? Without telling me?'

'Yes, it all happened very quickly. His butler died and he was very upset. He's gone on a voyage.'

'Well, I could look after the house while he's away.'

'No, Lizzie. Your place is here with Reuben and your baby.'

'He's not my baby. He belongs to the Devil. Oh Bobby, I gave birth to the son of the Devil.'

'Don't be silly. What are you talking about?'

His question went unanswered as if she was in another world. He looked round the kitchen. The wooden cradle that Reuben had made for the baby was empty and pushed into a corner of the room. He could not understand what was happening. *Son of the Devil, what does she mean?* She wasn't making any sense.

'Is there any more of that cheese?' she asked.

'Never mind the cheese, where's the baby?'

'He's gone.'

'What do you mean, he's gone?'

'I've given him to the Devil.'

Bobby sat on the edge of the bed and took hold of her shoulders. He looked straight into her eyes. She looked away and grinned, as if she were playing a game. Is *it a game she's playing or is it something much more serious?* He could not decide. He had always thought of Lizzie as a sensible person, always admired her for her resilience; she had never been melodramatic like this. He wished Reuben were here.

'Look at me, Lizzie,' he said, gripping her tightly. 'Tell me exactly what you've done.'

'He wouldn't stop crying. I shook him and he cried even more so I wrapped him up and took him up to the top of the moor. I put him where the Devil would find him, and take him. If the crows find him first they'll peck his eyes out like they do to the dead lambs.'

'Are you playing games with me, Lizzie? This is serious, tell me the truth.'

'I'm telling you the truth. He's up on the moor.'

'Oh, my God. Which part of the moor? Tell me, Lizzie, where exactly on the moor?'

'I can't remember, but I found a nice soft spot for him. He stopped crying when I put him down.'

Bobby threw her back on to the pillow, headed quickly for the door, and came face to face with Mrs Dawson just as she was walking in.

'I've called for my money,' she said.

Bobby pushed her aside, knocking her backwards against the open door. 'Get out of my way.'

'Well I never, there's no need for that,' said Mrs Dawson. 'I only want what's due to me for my trouble and effort. After all, I was here all through the night. That bairn would have died if it weren't for me.'

Bobby was not listening. He was halfway round the path girdling the cottage. 'Look after Lizzie, she's gone raving mad,' he shouted and continued racing up the track on to the moor.

The moor covered a large area and he searched for a long time, thrashing among the bracken and heather trying to keep calm and not cover the same places twice. In the distance he could hear the dog barking and thought it was in pursuit of a rabbit, but then decided that the barking was going on too long. The dog was an expert hunter and should have caught his quarry by now.

He walked in that direction and thought he heard the faint cry of the baby, or maybe he was mistaken and it was just a lamb bleating.

When the dog came into view he saw it was sat at the side of the little bundle, guarding it as if it were one of its own puppies. Approaching slowly he wondered if the dog would allow him to pick up the baby. It knew Bobby and was used to him taking rabbits from him, so he called the dog off to his side and patted it for its obedience. Gently picking up the crying baby and checking to see that no harm had come to it, he ran back to the cottage.

By the time Bobby got back with the baby, Annie had arrived and was in the kitchen with Lizzie and Mrs Dawson. A high-pitched argument between the three women was in full swing but stopped abruptly when he walked in. Mrs Dawson, not surprised at anything that was going on, took the baby from him, lovingly cradled it in her arms and instinctively exposed her breast. It snuggled up to her and fed clumsily, gulping noisily, the fullness of her breast making the feeding easier. Bobby, mystified, went off to see to the animals, leaving the three women to sort out their differences. They stared suspiciously at each other as the silence refuelled the argument. Exhausted from crying, the baby soon fell asleep and the shouting continued.

It was just a jumble of voices gaining no result until Annie, usually quietly spoken, thumped on the table and shouted, 'Stop it,' at the top of her voice. Then, when all was calm, she tried being philosophical, taking Lizzie's hand in hers and speaking softly.

'The baby is your responsibility, Lizzie. Look at the poor mite. You can't just abandon him.'

'I can and I will. If you leave him here alone with me I'll smother him with my pillow. Anyway, I'm leaving this place. I might even leave Dindley.'

'And where do you reckon you'll go?' asked Annie.

Lizzie shrugged her shoulders, unable to answer. She had not thought that far ahead but her reckless remark gave her the idea that she might do just that. *Why not?* she thought. *I can* go anywhere.

'You can have him. Take him, seeing as you're so concerned for his wellbeing. I give him to you.'

Before Annie could answer, Bobby returned. The animals were all fed and watered, and he just caught the end of Lizzie's remark. He could not understand why Lizzie was acting so strangely and why she wanted to give her baby away. It was so unlike her, she was usually so sensible. Mrs Dawson explained that it was quite common for a woman soon after giving birth to not be in her right mind, and took great pleasure in relating weird and wonderful tales of such cases she had heard about.

'You can't leave the bairn here. She'll kill him one way or another,' said Mrs Dawson.

'I suppose I could take him for a short while. That is, just until Lizzie's feeling better,' said Annie. 'Though never having had a child of my own I'll be at a loss as to how to look after him.'

'Give him to me. I'll take him,' Mrs Dawson said.

'Oh, no, Mrs Dawson. This is a family matter and I'm sure you have your hands full already with your own large family,' said Annie, hoping to keep the situation private and not wanting any scandal.

'One more won't make any difference to my brood and it could be some time before Lizzie's better.'

Both women knew the real reason why Lizzie was acting so defiantly, but neither let on to the other that they knew of the circumstances.

'Give him here,' said Mrs Dawson, gathering up her belongings and the baby and setting off down the lane. Annie disapprovingly trotted after her, leaving Bobby in the cottage with Lizzie.

Bobby paced the floor, Lizzie sat on the bed gazing into space. It was some time before they spoke. So much to say but where to start?

'What's going on, Lizzie?' Bobby asked quietly. 'This isn't like you at all.'

His sincerity gave Lizzie a feeling of closeness, a feeling she had not felt for anyone for many years. He had a way of making her open up and tell him her troubles and it was not long before she related the whole story. The terror of the rape. How Annie had conferred with her to conceal it so that the brothers would not fight and maybe one kill the other. How hard it had been to deceive Reuben all these months.

He pondered for a while, realising the gossip he had heard was true and he should have listened to his mother, but he still wanted to be strong and support Lizzie. He tried to find the right thing to say, thinking his feeble words would be inadequate.

'Why didn't you tell me, Lizzie?'

'I couldn't. Nobody had to know. It was a secret between Annie and me.'

'Does anyone apart from Annie know? Does Mrs Dawson know?'

'No. You mustn't tell anyone. Least of all Reuben. Just let them all think I've gone crazy.'

But Mrs Dawson did know and it would not be long before the whole village knew too.

Chapter 24

Two weeks later, Reuben returned home. Aggressive military life had not suited him and he looked dishevelled. He had not found a niche in the regiment where he comfortably fitted in, nor had he mixed easily with the other men or shown any valour. His concern for Lizzie, whom he thought was so near her confinement, and the attention he should have been giving to his newborn lambs had occupied his mind to the point where he could not concentrate on the military training. It came as a relief when he was granted a special dispensation to return home early on the understanding that he was to be called upon to return at a later date. He had left in such haste that he had forgotten to hand in the Baker rifle he had been issued with, and it was still slung over his shoulder as he happily walked up the lane to the cottage.

Lizzie had planned the meeting, his return, and what she would say. When the day was near for him to come home she would scrub the floors, clean and tidy everywhere, collect fragrant herbs, bathe and look attractive. She would put food on the table and, after he had eaten and rested, she would explain quietly about the baby and why she had given it away. Tell him how desperate she had felt and persuade him that she had done the right thing. She was sure he would be understanding.

She was standing in the kitchen, skinning and gutting a rabbit the dog had caught and had carried into the cottage when the door burst open and Reuben walked in. Her hands were all bloody and smelled of entrails, and her apron, on which she had repeatedly wiped her hands, was badly stained. She had rabbit blood on her face where she had rubbed her nose when it itched. The cottage was untidy and the animals yet to be fed.

'Reuben, what are you doing here? I wasn't expecting you back home yet, not for days.'

'I've rushed home to be with you for the birth of the baby but I can see it's already been born.'

'Yes, I'm relieved, more than you know, that it's all over,' she said.

'That's good. I hope you didn't suffer too much discomfort.'

'I was so frightened and in so much pain that Mrs Dawson stayed with me all night. And Annie came the next day and stayed for a short while,' she said, putting the rabbit joints into a pot of water boiling on the fire, washing her hands, and discarding the dirty apron. She pushed her uncombed hair back from her face, tossed her head back, smoothed her dress, and hoped she did not look too unkempt.

'Oh, you know I dislike that woman, but I suppose she has her uses. And the baby, is it all right?'

'It's a boy. I believe they've called him Samuel.'

'They?'

'Yes, Mrs Dawson named him.'

'Samuel? What sort of a name is that and what's it got to do with her? I should be the one to name my child. A family name. Where is he?'

'I gave him to her. I didn't want him. She fed him and took him.'

'What? My son with that wretched woman? Lizzie, are you crazy? What on earth did you do that for?'

'You left me here alone. You should have been here to look after me,' she said, forgetting all the words of explanation she had prepared.

'Surely I don't have to give a reason why. You know I had no choice. I had to go away. Anyway, it sounds as if you were looked after. You were all right without me.'

'No I wasn't. I've been to the gates of Hell and back. Reuben, believe me, that baby is the son of the Devil. You have no idea what it was like for me,' Lizzie said, becoming very flustered and laying the grounds for yet another bitter furore.

'So you gave him away. My son being given away. I can't believe what I'm hearing.'

'He's not your son,' she blurted out. 'He's Jack's son.' *Oh dear,* she thought. Frustration and temper were taking over, out of control. It was all coming out totally wrong, the wrong words just seemed to be escaping from her mouth. That was the last thing she'd wanted to say.

'You and Jack? Tell me, Lizzie, you don't mean that.'

'Yes I do, the baby's Jack's.'

Before she could explain what had happened, a hand came up from nowhere and caught her across her face. She reeled over and landed in a heap on the floor. Never before in her life had she been struck with such force. Shocked and frightened, she ran into the scullery and found sanctuary in the small, dusty space between the loom and the wall.

'You trollop, you disgust me,' he shouted, picked up his gun, loaded it, stormed out of the door, and raced down the lane to find Jack.

When he got to the forge the big doors were closed. He cupped his hands on the glass in the window and looked through. There was no fire burning, no activity at all, and the paddock was empty. He went to the house and banged on the door but it was locked and all the windows were shuttered.

'Come on out, you coward, you can't hide from me,' Reuben shouted. When there was no response he ran through the village waving the gun, like the head of an invading army. Villagers gathered their children and ran inside their homes for safety. He headed for his sister's house.

'Reuben, you'll wake the dead banging on my door like that. For goodness' sake get inside,' Annie said, giving him a push and quickly closing the door after him.

'What's going on?' asked Reuben. 'The forge is closed.'

'What are you doing with that gun? Give it to me.'

'No. If what Lizzie tells me is true I'm going to blow his brains out and hers as well. Where is he?'

'What has Lizzie told you?'

'That all this time she's been carrying on with Jack behind my back.'

'I'm sure she didn't say that. Calm down and listen to me. Your temper is getting the better of you. You're wrong. It wasn't like that at all. In fact he took her by brute force and raped her. Just once. A frail girl like Lizzie can't stand up to a violent man of that stature. Can't you see? It was one of his weapons to get back at you, and Lizzie has taken the brunt of this family's arguments. It's abominable that this could happen. This family should be ashamed of how we've treated her. It wasn't Lizzie's fault. She's the victim in all this. It cut me to the heart to see her so upset all these months.'

'You knew, didn't you? You're as bad as them. Why didn't you tell me?'

'Because I knew what you would do. Exactly what you are trying to do now, and one of you would have ended up dead. It was hard to know what to do for the best.'

'Where is he? I'll kill him.'

'He's gone. The bailiffs took charge of the forge because he didn't raise the money for the rent. Nobody in the village would back him because of the way he treated Lizzie, so he's fled.

'You mean everyone in the village knew about this? Am I the last to know?'

'They've only just found out because Mrs Dawson had to explain why she has the baby.'

'That woman. She'll be delighting in all this gossip. Where will I find Jack now then?'

'If you calm down I'll tell you. I believe he's gone to work in an iron foundry somewhere in Lancashire making machinery for the mills.'

'Who's got the forge now then?'

'Nobody. You'll be pleased to know that the Learoyds' solicitor has instructions to give you first chance. They know why you had to leave the forge when Father died and what a dedicated craftsman you are. So, my dear brother, it's yours if you want it. At an agreeable rent of course.'

'But I haven't got enough money for the rent. It's a wild dream I can't afford.'

'I'll lend it to you. I'm sure we can come to some amicable arrangement for repayment.'

Reuben wandered around the room, hands in his pockets, stamping his feet. 'Damn, damn,' he mumbled repeatedly, trying to make his mind up what to believe and what to do. Just when everything had been starting to come right, so much had gone wrong.

He was thoughtful for some time but slowly began to see reason. He felt the anger beginning to subside as he contemplated the future that was being offered to him. *It was such a mistake rushing into this marriage*, he thought, *but married I am and I must do right by Lizzie*. It was already evening and he still had a lot to do before nightfall.

'I best go and see Mrs Dawson,' he said.

'Don't go in anger, Reuben. I know she's gossiped, but she's been the rod and staff in all this. Lizzie and the baby could both have died had it not been for her. Putting the baby with her is our best answer to this problem.'

'No, I'll do what's best. I'm going to tell her she can keep the baby, as long as that's what Lizzie wants. Here, take the gun. It has to be handed in to the squire. Give it to Tom next time he visits. He can hand it in for me.'

After Reuben had gone she took the gun, carefully placed it out of sight in a drawer, and covered it with some of her petticoats. It would be safe there until Tom was able to collect it.

Reuben returned home about two hours later. He had almost skipped up the lane, unable to wait to tell Lizzie his good news. What a wonderful opportunity this would be to put all their troubles behind them. How they could now leave the desolate farm and enjoy life living in the smithy's house on the side of the forge. It would seem like luxury after the draughty old cottage on North Fell.

He would not have to sit at the loom weaving until the early hours of the morning trying to produce enough cloth to compete with the big mills that were being built in most valleys and towns. It would not be long before there would be one built in Dindley and they would need tools that he could make in the forge. He would have plenty of work and Lizzie could work in the mill. They would soon be able to repay Annie. It would be a brand new start.

Of course he thought he would have to apologise to Lizzie first and promise never to show anger towards her again. There would be no more quarrelling. He would not be able to tell her that he loved her, he wouldn't know how to say that. He didn't know the right words, but he would find ways of showing her.

'Lizzie, Lizzie. Where are you?' he shouted, bursting through the door unable to contain his excitement.

Lizzie had seen him running up the lane, had misunderstood his urgency and feared for her safety. She had pushed herself back into the small space behind the loom, out of sight, too frightened to move, imagining Jack with his head blown off, the constable chasing Reuben for the murder, and it all being her fault.

The long journey home from the militia had been without food, and all the ensuing turmoil had made Reuben very hungry. The rabbit stew cooking on the fire smelled good and he helped himself to a large portion. After he had eaten that, he filled his plate again with a second helping and Lizzie listened from her hideaway to the spoon scraping the tin plate. He had enjoyed it so much he circled his tongue round the plate until he had licked it clean. Lizzie waited some time after he had finished eating before thinking of leaving her hiding place. The room was quiet and she thought maybe he would be better tempered now he had eaten and rested, and she could try to talk to him. She wriggled from the tight space and found Reuben staring into space, a peculiar look on his face. He tried to talk to her but could not move his mouth and his head began to twitch. Her first reaction was to suspect that he was drunk, or was it his temper whelming up in him? She did not know what to do, whether to wait for him to speak or to hide again. Leaning against the far wall she watched him and his unusual behaviour and thought maybe now was the right time to try to explain.

'I know you must despise me, Reuben, but please try to understand it wasn't my fault,' she said.

She waited for a reply but froth came from his mouth when he tried to speak and he had difficulty breathing. She could see he was very ill so she rummaged around in her medicine cupboard, wondering which of her mixtures to give him. She had never seen anyone with these symptoms before, so for the time being she made a mild brew from camomile flowers and would refer to her book later for something more potent. Lizzie put the drink on the table in front of him but Reuben's whole body was now jerking so much he was unable to grasp the cup to drink. With one strong convulsion he arched his back and fell from the chair on to the floor and remained in that position; rigid and unconscious. Saliva dribbled from his mouth and his eyes were wide open, unblinking.

'Talk to me, Reuben, say something, please forgive me,' Lizzie said, shaking his shoulders. Dazed, frightened, her heart thumping in her chest, she knelt on the floor and cradled his head in her lap. Unable to accept the ghastly thought that he might be dead it was some time before the stark reality became apparent. Putting her hands on his face she closed his eyelids.

Chapter 25

Dindley was usually a sleepy hamlet where life carried on monotonously with the season after season routine, so any diversion from the humdrum existence was regarded with great excitement. Today was one of those days and inquisitive villagers, absent from their work, had come out of their homes and crowded the drovers' road. The alehouse, where even the women had been allowed inside to witness justice being done, was filled to capacity. Those at the back of the room and in the doorway jostled and pushed with their elbows to get a better view of this extraordinary event.

The constable, the rector and two parish councillors, all dressed in their official outfits, were assembled to adjudicate the meeting and sat squeezed on a settle along one wall. A long discussion had carried on between them as to the format the court of law should follow. There were to be two hearings today, the second one was of such great importance that they thought they may not be sufficiently competent to deal with it. A table in front of them was covered with official looking papers listing rules and regulations as a guidance to aid the proceedings.

'Can we start with the case of Mrs Ada Dawson and Mrs Clara Saunders each accusing the other of assault? Can they be brought to the front?'

The two women were pushed forward from somewhere in the middle of the crowded room, each with a defiant glare at the other and protesting loudly at being manhandled. The outcome of an argument that had got out of hand was now the basis of their court appearance and they continued to quarrel with each other as they stood in front of the table.

'Silence,' demanded the constable. 'You're both like a pair of fishwives. Mrs Dawson, can we hear from you first?'

'Yes. On Wednesday I went to her house,' she said, pointing at Mrs Saunders, 'and asked for the money she owed me for the bread my son had delivered over the past two weeks. She would not give me the money and called me a rogue because she said I'd charged her for bread she'd not had. I hadn't charged her too much and we had a row and she hit me in the face.'

'I did not hit her,' interrupted Mrs Saunders. 'It was her that hit me. She was in a very bad temper and she hit me calling me a low wicked woman.'

The two parish councillors agreed that this was a paltry matter for such a court and referred to the rector, asking if he would like to administer more worthwhile religious guidance to the two women. The rector nodded his approval and called it a disgraceful sinful thing when neighbours could not live in peace. The bench agreed that the case be dismissed and the second investigation be started.

'Please bring forward Elizabeth Webster.'

The crowd hushed and parted to leave a small corridor for Lizzie, who was brought out from a side room, to enter the alehouse court. Held firmly on each arm by volunteer helpers who wanted to be part of this eventful happening, she stood in a prominent position in front of the table facing the panel who were to judge her.

'Elizabeth Webster, widow of this parish, you have been brought here before this court because it is our belief that you wilfully administered poison to your husband, causing his instant death,' said the constable.

'No, no, I didn't. I wouldn't do such a thing.' Lizzie tried to plead her innocence but a loud buzz erupted from the crowd and cries of 'witch' and 'murderer' resonated round the room, drowning out her feeble voice. The constable, who was new to his position, pulled at the neck of his ill-fitting uniform and called the meeting to order.

'It is well known that for some time you have prepared mixtures of a suspicious nature and although, it must be said, cures for certain maladies were sometimes achieved it remains unknown how many people you might have harmed.'

Lizzie again pleaded with them that she had not committed such a terrible crime and looked round the room desperate to find a friendly face, but all she saw were pointing fingers and accusing nods even from those who had benefited from her medicines. They had already deemed her guilty. The hearing was progressing so quickly and noisily that the rector, appointed to take notes of the proceedings, could not write fast enough to record all the events. The pen dipped in and out of an ink well at great speed, the ink staining his fingers and smudging the page. He hoped the report would be reasonably legible.

'I thought you were my friends and now you've all become my enemies. I only ever wanted to help those of you who were suffering. How can you all think so little of me?' she asked, but her plea went unheard.

The constable banged on the table to bring the meeting to order once again. 'It is apparent that you had differences with the deceased, your husband, concerning the parentage of your child which was the result of an unfaithful act with another man. Bitter arguments took place between you and the deceased and you took your evil revenge in the way you knew best by poisoning him.'

Hoping he had enough resources and evidence to bring the hearing to a quick end, the constable looked gravely at Lizzie and the room hushed. He spoke slowly and said each word clearly.

'For your unforgivable sins you will be taken from here immediately to Ripon Liberty Prison with instructions to await a future trial in the high courts.'

'No,' she shouted. 'I'm not leaving here. I will fear for my life in such a place. Please, listen to me. You don't know what really happened. He didn't drink the medicine.'

'Tell it to the court,' came a raucous shout from the crowded room.

Anxious to return to his farm, and still needing to escort Lizzie to

Ripon, the constable rose to his feet, raised his arm and announced, 'The business of the day is ended to our satisfaction. Please rise from your seats and go about your daily toils. Those of you with a thirst may now be served. Landlord, you may take over.'

There were no windows, just a small grille in the door letting in a narrow beam of light. The smell was overbearing; a mixture of urine, vomit and body odours permeated the prison van. It travelled at breakneck speed and Lizzie, sure she was being delivered into the jaws of Hell, was thrown from side to side in the confined space.

Bruised physically and mentally, her arrival at the prison was a stupefying experience. She sat on the stone floor, her back against the wall, bewildered, the bang of the big door and the sound of the key turning in the lock ringing in her ears, her continued pleas that she was innocent totally ignored. Still nobody would listen to her that she was not a criminal or vagrant to be incarcerated in such a frightening cold, damp place. She could not believe that God would punish her so cruelly.

It took a while for her eyes to become accustomed to the dark. In the gloom she could see a child of about eight years old hunched up in one corner, dirty and dressed in rags, and continuously whimpering. In another corner an old woman was muttering to herself and smirked mockingly as she hobbled over to where Lizzie was sitting and pulled at her clothes looking for anything she could snatch.

'Did ya bring any food with ya, love?' she cackled. Her teeth were black and her bad breath made Lizzie flinch.

'Get away from me, you old hag.'

'Oh yeah, Miss High and Mighty. I've seen your sort before. You're no bleeding well better than the rest of us now you're in 'ere. Come on, let's see what you've got then, love.'

They rolled on the floor, grabbing whatever and pulling hair until Lizzie, being the stronger and the old woman being weak from months of imprisonment, took the upper hand. Empty handed, the old woman scurried back to her corner.

The silence returned, only broken by the sound of sobbing from the young girl. Lizzie beckoned the child to come to her and instinctively hugged her tightly as much to comfort herself as the child. It reminded her of her young siblings and how she used to console them when they were ill or had fallen while playing. How she wished she could return to those happy days with her father, who'd had great expectations for her future, always there to give guidance and instruction, and her mother's influence teaching them what was wrong and what was right. She thought of the evenings when they would all sit round the fire and sing songs together; her mother suggesting hymns and her father wanting the slightly risqué songs that would make them all laugh. There was no music in this place and no ally she could turn to for help. The thought that these intimidating surroundings, this dank and dangerous place was now to be her life, filled Lizzie with dread. Maybe the hanging, which she felt sure would be her fate, would be better than this.

It was not long before she was taken to a bathhouse, stripped of her clothes, put into a lukewarm bath and scrubbed. After being examined for lice, she was given an overall to wear and isolated behind a locked door in a cell.

Chapter 26

The key rattled in the lock and the door opened.

'Visitor for you,' said the prison warden and the door banged closed, locking the visitor in with Lizzie and the sound of the impact resonating inside the cell. The Reverend Sewell polished his spectacles and placed them back on the end of his long nose. Peering over them he viewed the small cell in which Lizzie had been confined in isolation. He looked up to the small window high in one wall, too high to look through and which let in very little sunlight, but what little there was cast shadows on the ceiling. Lizzie had spent hours watching the shapes slowly moving across the ceiling as the sun orbited in its path.

At night the moonlight did the same, and night after night Lizzie had lain awake watching the patterns and trying to make pictures. It reminded her of happier days at her childhood home when she would sit round the hearth with her family and make pictures in the glowing fire. She tried to make herself think of her childhood days to take her mind off this terrible place she was unable to escape from, but when she thought of her home in Herefordshire she could not escape the image of the disastrous blaze.

The other two walls of the cell were whitewashed; stark and oppressive. Set in the fourth wall was a big wooden door; its opening and closing controlled by the uncompassionate key holder. There was no furniture, just a stone shelf built against one of the walls for her to sleep on. Lizzie had asked if the young girl she had met when she first arrived, might be put in the cell with her, as much for her own sanity as the child's, but Lizzie was considered far too dangerous to have company. Nobody would listen to her; she had been condemned as guilty before any trial and was becoming resigned to the fact that there was no way out of this. It would be the end of her short life.

She sat on the stone bed, her legs dangling over the side and her head bowed, staring despairingly at the floor. She did not look up to greet her visitor; she knew who it was, she recognised the long feet splayed out like a fish's tail.

'You're my first visitor. Four weeks I've been here, shut up in this dreadful place.'

'Well, this is a monstrous thing that you have done. You must take your punishment,' said the rector.

'Have you come to help me get out of here or have you come to seal my fate?' She felt very brazen with her reply but did not care any more; this was her life she was fighting for.

'Neither. I've come to pray with you and help you redeem your soul.'

'I need Mr Fothergill here to help me. He'd believe I'm innocent. Can you contact him for me?'

'I cannot burden him with your problems. He knows nothing of your evil ways, nor shall he. The object of his travelling is to recuperate from his trauma and not be bothered with your tiresome affair.'

'Tiresome affair? This is no tiresome affair as far as I'm concerned,' Lizzie screeched.

'Try to calm yourself. The Devil has entered your body once again, Lizzie. The best thing you can do now is to pray.'

She *had* prayed, it was compulsory. Taken from her cell every morning and made to kneel with her eyes closed until she was allowed to move. After prayers the other inmates were taken to their daily work stations or classrooms but she was hastily returned to her cell and caged like a wild animal, the habitual sound of the door and lock ringing in her head. She had nothing to do but listen to noises. The sound of the wind, occasional hooves and wheels grating on the road outside or the birds singing. How lucky they were to be free. Some mornings, her so-called freedom from the isolation lasted longer because she was placed in a bath and degradingly scrubbed with carbolic soap until her skin was raw.

'Have you brought me any food?' Lizzie asked the rector.

'No. Is the food here not sufficient?'

'One bowl of gruel which tastes like cabbage water. Maybe a piece of bread if I've been obedient. Would you call that sufficient?'

'There are people who would be pleased to have even that,' said the rector.

'I can't eat anyway. I have no appetite. Nor can I sleep. The days and nights are long, empty hours.'

'Your time must be spent in prayer asking for forgiveness and hopefully for a lenient punishment.'

'Twice now someone has brought a basket of food in for me. They won't tell me who it is or allow me to see the person. Do you know who might care enough to do that?'

'No I don't, but obviously the Lord is answering your prayers and I will leave you in his hands. Remember, Lizzie, the power of prayer. Put your trust in God,' he said and laid his scrawny hand on her head before banging on the door to be released.

That night she lay on the hard bed watching the moon-washed shadows on the ceiling and tried to imagine who might be concerned enough to bring her a basket of food. She tried to form the shapes into a letter, a first letter of a name maybe or a face to give her a clue, but nothing transpired.

It could have been Annie. Annie knew the dreadful story of the rape and Lizzie's state of mind. Surely she would be sympathetic and stick by her and come forward to help. On the other hand, to keep up appearances, she would never admit to ever having known any of it.

There was Mrs Dawson, but she would not be able to make the long journey to the prison even for the gossip it would supply her with. Her family commitments, especially now with Samuel to look after as well as her own, were too demanding.

She thought of Bobby, hoping it would be him, but his mother would tell him to keep away and not get involved. *Is he man enough to reject her influence,* she wondered, *and make his own mind up?* She was saddened that she would never get the chance to thank him for being so kind to her when he had helped her in the cottage. How she might have died if he had not found her in the meadow that night when the baby was born. How she always enjoyed his visits and how fond she had become of him.

If only Mr Fothergill were here. He would know how to sort out this mess, but he did not even know of her predicament and she did not know how to contact him.

Day after day the routine seemed endless: prayers, baths, pictures on the ceiling and nobody listening to her pleading her innocence. Always awake waiting for the first sounds of the morning: the blackbirds singing, the cathedral bells ringing and the footsteps of the early workers.

The days turned into weeks and all she could think of was her mother and father and how she had wanted to be someone special and make them proud of her. How disappointed they would be if they could see her now and know how she had messed up her life.

She had just resigned herself to the ultimate punishment when the door banged open and she was taken from the cell. *This is it*, she thought and prepared herself for the worst, but she was handed a bundle of her belongings and told she was free to go. She could not understand and stood not knowing which way to go. She was pushed out of the front door on to the street. She stood gazing around, a horse and carriage blocking her view. *Where should I go?*

'Come on, jump up here,' the carriage driver shouted.

'Me? Do you mean me?' she asked, looking up and recognising Tom the gamekeeper.

'Yes you. I'm taking you home. Come on, quick, before they change their minds,' he said.

On the journey back to Dindley he related what had happened. 'The rabbit you cooked and Reuben ate was laced with poison but not by your hand. I had soaked a carcass in strychnine and put it down near the warren to kill a fox but your dog picked it up instead and brought it home to you. The rest of the rabbit stew was fed to the dog which howled for two hours and then died. Bobby recognised the symptoms as strychnine poisoning and realised what must have happened. He knew I was the only person who would handle strychnine and he demanded that I tell the constable what had happened. Bobby has strived long and hard to have you freed.'

'So was it Bobby who brought the baskets of food into the prison for me?'

'It was, but he wasn't allowed to see you because he was too militant in fighting for your release.'

'Please don't take me back to Townsend Cottage. I couldn't bear to step inside that place anymore.'

'No, don't worry. You're going to stay with Bobby's family. Mrs Saunders says you can stay with them until you decide what your future is to be.'

'I haven't thought about a future. I thought my life was over.'

As the horse trotted down the drovers' road, reducing speed as it approached its destination, Lucy came running up to the carriage. 'Lizzie, Lizzie, you're going to share my bedroom. Won't that be wonderful? We can pretend you're my big sister.'

'I would like that very much,' Lizzie said, jumping down to the ground that she thought she would never tread again. 'I used to have a sister. Come, let's go in and I'll tell you all about her.'

Mrs Saunders, feeling guilty that she had done her fair share of gossiping and not supported Lizzie in her plea of innocence, looked up from the kitchen table where she was working and managed an involuntary smile. Her house was a happy, caring home with no quarrelling and she meant to keep it that way. Lizzie was to be under no illusion that she was there to get revenge or to cause any trouble.

'You're very welcome in my home, Lizzie,' she explained, 'but I'm not a charity and you'll have to find work straight away and pay your way.'

Lizzie was humbled. It was an odd feeling; a sense of relief, torn between tears and laughter.

Guiseppe Villa
Rome

July 8th 1830

The Rev. Augustus Sewell

Reverend Sir,

At last I have reached my desired destination. The journey was pleasant enough, just one or two mishaps encountered along the way but swiftly overcome. I was thankful of the lodges you recommended. I found them to be more than satisfactory especially the one in Paris.

I have now found a gentlemen's boarding rooms on the outskirts of Rome where the food is palatable and the wine flowing. My fellow lodgers are amiable and conduct interesting conversations and pastimes. The climate is a sheer indulgence to be enjoyed each and every day. There is much here to appreciate and my state of mind is calming slowly but not yet recovered sufficiently to face the long journey home. Taking all this into consideration I think my sojourn will be continued here for some time to come.

Your last letter was forwarded to me here and I was distressed to read of Reuben Webster's death. It appears to have been a most disagreeable affair. I have written to my solicitor with instructions to give guidance to Lizzie regarding her property and for her future welfare.

Thank you for looking after my affairs in Dindley and I hope it will be no trouble for you to continue on my behalf for the time being.

Fothergill

Chapter 27

The river, calmly snaking ever onwards, reflecting the golden edged silver clouds like a mirror, now fed the waterwheel of a flax mill, newly built, further down the valley. A new row of cottages, built on the edge of the village, housed migrant workers and early every morning Lizzie joined the spinners and linen weavers for the trek to the mill. The sun was almost up and long shadows slanted across the ground. The work at the mill was hard, noisy and crowded, and the other girls were antagonistic towards her and provoked arguments which erupted without reason. She still, even after proven to be innocent, carried the stigma of her husband's death. Lizzie hated every minute of every long working day there.

Breakfast in the Saunders' house was usually a rushed affair, everything laid out on the table and everyone grabbing what they could and then straight out of the door for the walk to whatever work they had, but this morning Lizzie was loitering.

'Hurry up, Lizzie, you'll be late,' said Mrs Saunders.

'I'm not going,' said Lizzie, circling the spoon slowly round her dish of porridge.

'Why's that? Are you not well?'

'Yes, I am very well. I just feel that I cannot work one hour longer in that place. I'm not going back there ever again.'

She had enjoyed her stay with the Saunders family, but it was now starting to feel intrusive and she thought it was time to pack her bags and move on. But where was she to go? Where would she work? A decision had to be made. She could go back to Townsend Cottage or work in the kitchen at the big house or maybe go back home to Hereford, but none of these options inspired her. She had no interest in her life which seemed as empty and dry as a desert. While considering all her choices, a knock came at the door. A boy had run down from the high road with a letter that had arrived on the mail coach. He waited for a remuneration but was unlucky because Mrs Saunders knew he would have been paid by the coach driver.

'It's for you, Lizzie.'

Lizzie looked at the letter for some time, surprised that anyone should write to her. The scroll writing on the front was, without doubt, her name and, suspecting it could only be bringing bad news, from which she had now become almost immune, she laid it on the table unopened.

'Well open it,' said Mrs Saunders, who had never had a letter delivered to her door before and was so curious she was almost opening it herself.

'It's from Mr Fothergill's solicitor,' said Lizzie. 'They want to see me. I'm to go to their office in Harrogate on Tuesday afternoon.'

Pipe tobacco filled the air and dark furniture, wooden panelling covered all the walls, and half-drawn heavy curtains which blocked out most of the light made the solicitor's office a gloomy, airless place. The smell, like a tomb just reopened, hit the back of Lizzie's throat. She sat in awe, hands folded on her lap, tongue-tied and too shy to speak while dour looking lawyers, unconcerned with her presence, carried on the meeting as if she were invisible. She was pleased the rector had accompanied her as chaperon as he was able to speak, with confidence, on her behalf.

To her surprise the meeting was in her favour. Mr Fothergill had given instructions that Townsend Cottage, the grazing land and livestock were to be sold. Firstly to be offered to the new mill owner who would more than likely pay the most profitable price. The revenue was to be invested securely to give Lizzie an annual income. As he was to stay in Italy for the time being, Lizzie was to live in his house and oversee the management of his property. A small allowance was to be paid to her from the estate of the late Miss Dorothea Fothergill.

On the return journey to Dindley, sitting side by side in the carriage without having to guiltily look Lizzie straight in the eye, the rector took the opportunity to talk to her and try to turn her good luck to his own advantage.

'Well, Lizzie, you've had more than your fair share of sorrow in your life, but now you must use what the Lord has given you and find peace by bestowing some of your fortune upon others.'

'I wouldn't exactly call it a fortune and it'll be a long time before I can do that. I will never forget the people who turned against me. Even you thought I was guilty. I really thought I was to die for something I hadn't done. The only option you gave me was to pray.'

'You must put your grief behind you, Lizzie. Your prayers have been answered as I knew they would be and now you must repay His blessing.'

'And how do I do that?'

'Maybe you could use a room in the house, occasionally, to feed the less fortunate children of the village. The temptation of a bowl of broth would bring them together and then I could instruct them in the ways of the Lord.'

'I'll think about it, but there's something I must do first at Townsend Cottage,' said Lizzie, reluctant to be too forthcoming. It was not a question of whether she would do it. She knew she would, but she'd had enough of trying to please other people, from now on she was going to be in control. The rector must wait for his answer.

It was a balmy evening. The bees were still busy collecting nectar from the abundance of late summer flowers growing among the lush grass in the meadow. Lizzie could smell the fragrance and hear the constant buzz of the worker bees as she walked slowly up the track to North Fell. Memories came flooding back into her mind, some good but mostly bad. There was only one occasion she could remember when she thought she really loved Reuben, and that was why she was here.

The cottage door was wide open, which was unusual because she had left it secure, but of course that had been weeks ago. She could hear someone moving about inside and was annoyed to think that someone was living in her house without permission. There was a lot of banging and, being alone with no companion, she became fearful of who it might be.

'Hello,' she shouted round the edge of the door.

No answer came but the banging continued and the sound of things falling on the floor was alarming. With trepidation she ventured inside and jolted to a stop as she almost trod on a grass snake; its green-ringed body coiled on the dusty floor. She heard bleating in the kitchen and saw a lamb, frightened and frantically jumping against the wall trying to find a way out, but the snake was blocking its escape route.

Lizzie ran out to find a stick but the ones on the ground were thin and pliable and of no use. She had to break a branch from a tree to get one with sufficient strength to hold the slippery creature. It obligingly curled round the stick and she headed, stick in hand, for the meadow, but as soon as the snake started to unravel itself she dropped it, pointing it in the direction of the river. Back at the cottage the lamb had found its way out and was running briskly up the track towards the moor.

Lizzie stretched up and felt along the hammer beam. The dust made her sneeze, but yes it was still there, the thing she had come for. The candle box holding the cherished key.

Four winters passed. The arrangement with the rector worked amicably; not only did the children receive religious enlightenment, but Lizzie was also able to teach them to read and write. The house had turned into a practical school with children from the village and the mill workers' cottages attending regularly.

Today a new pupil, a five-year-old boy, nervously stood at the door. 'Come in,' Lizzie shouted. 'Join the other children. What's your name?'

'Samuel Dawson,' the child said quietly.

'Samuel? I didn't recognise you.'

'I'm different. I used to have a broken lip, but I've been away and a man mended it.'

'Well, I think you are now the most handsome young man I have ever seen. I would like you to sit here next to me.'

* * *

Reviews

If you enjoyed *Ribbon of River* please consider leaving a rating and review on Amazon – all genuine comments and feedback are welcome and very much appreciated. Thank you.

Acknowledgements

With thanks to Bernie Crosthwaite for her encouragement to keep writing and friends at Knaresborough writers' group for their feed back. Also to Karen Perkins for the editorial.

For more information about Rose Marie Shaw and Ribbon of River, please visit:

www.lionheartgalleries.co.uk

LionheART Publishing House

For all your publishing needs.

Services include:

Copyediting
Proofreading
Formatting
Cover Design and Creation
Book Trailers

www.lionheartgalleries.co.uk
publishing@lionheartgalleries.co.uk
www.facebook.com/LionheartPublishing
@LionheartG

An imprint of LionheART Galleries

Printed in Great Britain
by Amazon